•

Lovers & Oth

Lovers & Other Strangers

Carol Malyon

CANADIAN CATALOGUING IN PUBLICATION DATA

Malyon, Carol, 1933-
Lovers & other strangers

ISBN 0-88984-169-1

I. Title. II. Title: Lovers and other strangers.

PS8576.A5364L6 1996 C813'.54 C95-933211-1
PR9199.3.M35L6 1996

Published by The Porcupine's Quill, Inc., 68 Main Street, Erin, Ontario NOB 1TO with financial assistance from The Canada Council and the Ontario Arts Council. The support of the Government of Ontario through the Ministry of Culture, Tourism and Recreation is also gratefully acknowledged, as is the support of the Department of Canadian Heritage through the Book and Periodical Industry Development Programme and the Periodical Distribution Assistance Programme.

Represented in Canada by the Literary Press Group. Trade orders are available from General Distribution Services.

Readied for the press by John Metcalf.
Copy edited by Doris Cowan.

Cover is after a photograph by Jenny Lynn/Graphistock.

For Adrian & for Marjory

Contents

A Meditation on Extinction

•

Pencils

•

•

IT IS EASY to read short stories. There are lots of them around. Some of them could be true; they could have happened already or be happening right now. At this moment perhaps someone is typing words about you reading the words upon this page. If you listen hard enough you might hear the clicking sound. Look around quickly; try to catch a flickered movement.

If you begin to read a story now, it will soon be over & you can start another. You already know this, of course; you have read short stories before. The ones in this book are very short. Skip through & check, if you don't believe me.

You finish a story, & put it down, as though it is merely a piece of fiction, as though the people disappear when you close the book, or as soon as the author stopped writing, as though they only exist inside the author's mind. As though the author is more real than the characters. As though you are.

You don't know the author. All the author intends to tell you is hidden inside the stories. Connect-the-dots. Join up the periods, & then the letters in between will fall in place. Connect-the-dots. See what you get.

Connect-the-dots. The author does it too, connects them with an electric typewriter or word processor until suddenly there's a power failure or the electricity is cut off. Then with a pencil.

Luckily the author has saved a pencil in case of an emergency like this. If the pencil's lost the story can't be written, & we need stories, to try to understand who we are.

For example, a man sits in a restaurant & talks of his father. This fascinates the woman who is with him. She has never understood men. They remind her of Russian dolls with painted faces, other dolls with painted faces hiding inside.

Mysteries. This man, who is already a father himself, talks of his own father as though there is something mysterious about fathering, as though being a father himself doesn't help, is irrelevant.

A woman listens. She has never been a father, has hardly known her own. Once she knew a man who fathered her children. At the time she thought she knew him well.

She remembers jokes around a board-room table:

I know her.

In the biblical sense?

Ha ha. Ha ha ha.

Guffaws from all the men in the room. She is a secretary & writes their words down. *Ha ha ha,* she records, being accurate. They wear their ordinary pleasant faces, but she remembers how they laugh. The secretaries compare stories at lunch time, & go back to their offices afterward, wearing ordinary faces also.

Of course the men talk this way. Older men taught them. Of course they ignore the secretary, although she is useful, the way a pencil is useful, the way, if the men tried to get along without them they would suddenly realize how much secretaries & pencils simplified their lives.

Imagine it. A world without pencils. Suddenly you wake up one morning & discover all the pencils have disappeared.

The man who is already a father wonders how he will ever explain to his children what a pencil used to be like. He could draw one to show them, if he had one to draw with. He will tell them: *We used them instead of machines; we could carry one in a pocket & use it anywhere, without batteries. The dark part in the centre made marks upon our pages. We used to call it lead but it was really graphite.*

Why didn't you call it graphite? they ask, being reasonable.

It was just part of the mythology that went with pencils, he says, mythology being the word he uses for whatever he doesn't know. *Let's look it up*, he says, but when they look in the encyclopedia they discover the reference to pencils has disappeared. Perhaps there never was one. After all, in those days everyone knew what a pencil was. They were so ordinary.

Perhaps the thought police removed all mention of pencils because they were subversive. You could use them to write anything you wanted, & people did.

People had dozens of them, he tells the children. *You could buy packages of them in the five & ten.*

What's a five & ten? they ask.

Perhaps some other time he'll tell them. Right now he doesn't want to get side-tracked away from pencils.

They came with different hardnesses of lead, he says.

You mean graphite, the children correct him, & the father says, *Yes, yes, but the name's not what's important. What matters is what the substance could do. Anyway* 2H *was very hard & made fine lines.* HB *was softer, didn't rip the page, & was easy to erase.*

What did the letters stand for? the children ask.

What letters?

The H *&* *the* B.

The man has no idea, so he tells about the little erasers instead, how they were fastened onto the end of the pencil with metal. *You couldn't lose them; as long as you had the pencil you had a tiny eraser handy, until it wore out.*

People kept losing their pencils, he tells them. *They'd put them down for a moment & forget where they'd left them. But it didn't matter. Every house had lots. There'd be another on a counter or in the back of a kitchen drawer or on a work-bench or in a pocket.*

Companies printed their names on pencils & handed them out free. Those were the days, he says. *Imagine a store just handing you a free pencil.* The children try to imagine this & can't. They can't even imagine a pencil. The man remembers that his father had a pencil with Imperial Coal printed on the side. The company he bought coal from must have given it to him. *What did he use coal for?* the children ask.

They lasted, he tells the children. *They didn't need servicing. They didn't dry out. They waited in a drawer until they were needed. Not deteriorating. Not getting rusty or mouldy or rotten. Those were the good old days,* he says, & watches their eyes glaze over at the phrase. Here he goes again, they're thinking. He knows this. He remembers being a kid, his father telling old stories that he's forgotten, as though this was a ritual task of fathers. If he could remember those stories now he might understand the man that he called father. If his father had written the stories down it would be a place to make a start.

When the man talks to his children, he tells them about the old days when there were pencils. When he talks to the woman he talks about his father who kept a pencil tucked above his ear. All carpenters did this, he remembers, & delivery men. Sometimes they wore caps. Perhaps they wore them to keep the pencils in place. He tries to remember about the caps to tell his children later. Probably he'll forget. Lately when he starts to tell them something, the words suddenly disappear. Perhaps this has always happened. He isn't sure. He thinks it is connected with missing pencils.

The words are disappearing, but not the thought that there are words he ought to say. He thinks, this is what it is to be expendable, like a pencil. Some day his children will try to describe him to their children. They will also be inarticulate. *If only we had one of those pencil-things the old man was always talking about, then we could write down his description or draw his picture.* He imagines how they will look when they say this, the way they'll laugh.

A man talks to a woman. He'll never be able to make her understand. Why does he bother? Why does she listen?

Words are hard to find. He looks them up. They still fit inside a dictionary; they no longer fit inside his mind. An emptiness is happening inside him & crowds them out. It takes up the same amount of space that once was filled with words. He feels this happen. It is a secret.

He is still trying to explain the fathering mystery.

The woman once had a father. She had grandfathers, brothers, uncles, male cousins. She could never understand them. She didn't like all the women in her family, but she could understand the way their minds worked. She couldn't escape their way of thinking; it was etched inside her brain like a tattoo. She understood the women, so they didn't interest her at all. She would like to understand the man across the table, but he is as inarticulate as all the other men who have ever touched her life.

These men, she thinks. It is as though they don't have words inside their heads, as though they reach for a word & it is gone. If they'd only written down their stories when they still knew them, we women could read them at our leisure, & begin to understand.

The man fumbles for memories & words. He uses cigarettes to do something with his hands, so the woman won't notice that he fumbles.

He has forgotten what he was talking about, like trying to touch summer in December, or childhood as an adult. Later he will try to remember this moment. He will grab at it & feel it disappear like cigarette smoke.

He had a father. He tries to remember what that was like. He reaches for a pencil before he remembers that pencils have disappeared. *The memory of pencils is disappearing,* he tells her. *I wanted to tell a story about them. I should have written it down sooner.*

•

The Mythologies of Lovers & Elephants…

•

•

•

Mythologies

•

•

WE CREATE OUR OWN MYTHOLOGIES. No one else can do it for us. For instance:

This is only the second time we make love but already we create stories. *Remember the first time we kissed?* you ask. *We were so shy at first*, I comment. We both lie.

Our first kiss? As if it matters. Our lips made physical contact last week, but we have known each other so long, so well. Our minds have always kissed, licked at each other, entangled, then pulled away, been drawn quickly back.

We hugged often to defuse the electricity that crackled around us. We cared for each other; we listened, & loved as good friends love. We shared our thoughts & dreams & memories. Our lips never touched, but what did it matter? Our minds touched. If we wanted to imagine ourselves kissing we could do so easily. We could imagine whatever we wanted.

Shy? We were never shy with each other. How could we be?

Last week we touched each other all over. It seemed so natural, as though we'd being doing it all along.

Perhaps we should have feared having our illusions shattered. We could so easily have been disappointed, our expectations so high, our imaginations so fertile. Could the reality of our coupling possibly equal the anticipation? Be as perfect as we'd already imagined?

It could. It was.

We were never shy. We groped toward each other & clung like drowning swimmers. There was no one else inside our ocean, no reason for modesty or inhibition. As though the world was ending anyway: what would the gods care whether we broke some silly societal rule?

Of course I remember our first kiss, I say. *We stood here in this doorway ...*

We will never be shy with each other again, you reassure me.

It goes on. We explore each other with our hands, our mouths, our tongues. Your cock discovers the inside of my body; the inside of my body discovers your cock. We explore, learn shapes & textures. Is there some part of you I haven't touched yet? Quick, let me find that place & explore it now.

We pretend this never happened until last week, that we haven't always explored each other, touched, moved away, then returned to touch again.

Some day we will have to explain this to our spouses, but later, much later. Right now we make love a second time, as we begin to count the way the world counts.

•

Somewhere a Piper Plays Elephant Songs

•

•

THERE ARE SO MANY things about elephants I haven't told you. Some of them are true; others happen inside dreams.

When elephants call to each other from a great distance the sound is too low for humans to hear. This is true. A newspaper clipping is pinned to my bulletin board which proves it. Once something is written on a page it becomes fact. I must be careful what I write down in this letter.

Elephants have copper eyes that glow in firelight, like those of cats along the highway reflecting headlights. They hate flashbulb photographs for this reason. Never startle elephants by taking flashbulb photos they're not expecting.

Elephants have baggy purple skin, as though huge mammoths began to diet & lost weight too suddenly. Folds of purple sag from their bodies & wobble as they walk. Drooping eyelids almost obscure their copper eyes. When ponderous elephant shapes lumber across the grassland, a dividing line disintegrates, no longer separates reality from dream.

Most people find elephant information difficult to accept. It doesn't matter. We can believe & believe until it's true, you in your city & I in mine, inside our different time zones. We have so much in common, you & I. Our love for elephants & for each other. We have our secrets, our stories. No one can touch them.

Elephants love bagpipe music. Everyone knows this. Pipers play in far-off Scotland to avoid them. All bagpipe players have heard of the Pied Piper, & his elephant story makes them nervous. How a herd of the beautiful creatures followed a piper through African plains. They criss-crossed back & forth, marching in one direction & then another. Other elephants heard the piping & ambled toward the sound; one after another they joined the procession.

The piper built enormous campfires each night & slept fitfully beside them. Copper elephant eyes glowed all around him, suspended in the dark. It became harder & harder for him to sleep. He grew irritable, developed headaches, indigestion, facial twitches. Each morning he discovered more & more elephants gathered around him. They stared at him & waited. He pretended to be asleep, but eventually had to stir, get up, stretch his arms toward the empty sapphire sky. He found it hard to urinate while hundreds of copper eyes were watching. Soon the elephants became restless & trumpeted angrily, until the piper picked up his bagpipe & started to play. Wild wailing music skirled around their magnificent heads & somehow calmed them.

Each morning the piper set out. Sometimes he backtracked along the path taken the day before, sometimes he intersected it & veered off in a new direction. He piped all day, & the herd of elephants followed behind him. No one came near them. They moved like a purple cloud across the grassland. Huge elephant feet kept time to *Road to the Isles* & *Bluebells of Scotland* & *Loch Lomond*. Their trunks swung back & forth as though they were dancing.

We know of elephants, you & I, their baggy purple skin, how they see the world through copper eyes; we know of their passion for bagpipe music. Perhaps this is all we can be sure of. We phone, write letters, meet when we can. We discuss elephants to avoid the deeper issues.

Reading an encyclopedia late one night I discover a reference to the gestation period of elephants & phone at 3 am to inform you.

Imagine, I say, *624 days! & it can extend as much as a hundred days longer!* We try to imagine this variation. A pregnant elephant carrying an infant inside her belly for an extra hundred days. More than three months! But talk of gestation is too erotic; we need to divert the conversation to a neutral topic. *Left- & right-handedness has been observed in elephants,* you tell me, & I'm amazed.

Your words are beautiful, as always. They travel across the country unaltered. I can imagine you are beside me, instead of a thousand miles away. We masturbate & talk. How long can this go on? we wonder.

The piper wonders the same thing. He heads in one direction or another, & wishes he had a compass or had orienteered with boy scouts when he was young. Africa is enormous. As a schoolboy he memorized continents in order of size, & remembers that only Asia is larger. He has no map, & no idea where he is. He knows the sun appears from the east in the morning & falls into the west every night. His dreams are of the sea; each morning he imagines where it is, then heads toward it.

We imagine each other, you & I. We imagine ourselves, & then the people we need in our lives. It is the only way we can survive. Every evening we lie down & enter our dreams; every morning we wake up & hope they continue. Time moves on, & we ..., we keep moving; we change direction every day like a lost piper who takes up his pipes again & begins to play. What else can he do?

•

… & Other Strangers

•

•

•

Bellefair

•

•

SARA BABYSITS HER FRIEND'S HOUSE, easily, as though she could move into some other life.

This is what it would be like to own these dishes, sit on this chair, eat at this table, read these books. This is what it would be like to own this cat: scoop canned cat food into the orange bowl, shake dry food into the beige one, pour fresh water into the brown. Open the back door to let it in or out. The cat flops at Sara's feet & rolls around, purring, *Pat me, pat me, pat me,* until Sara does. She listens to it purr. The sound is bigger than the cat. The rumble of trains across a trestle, of a man's voice late at night.

Instructions are everywhere, printed neatly on self-stick paper, yellow butterflies. Their wings rustle as Sara walks by: *Put out garbage Monday & Thursday, Push this button to pick up phone messages, Water plants once a week, The cat sometimes stays out all night.* Director's notes: *This is a role; here's how to act it.*

Lined up neatly on shelves are books Sara has always meant to read: the Bröntes, Cervantes, Flaubert, Henry James. A tattered volume of *Writers at Work: The Paris Review Interviews,* edited by George Plimpton, who can do anything, who could move into a house & act as though he'd always lived there.

George Plimpton interviews Sara: *You say you live here on*

Bellefair Avenue & are happy. Would you like to show us around the house? His voice sounds like Edward R. Murrow: *Sara. This is your life.*

Certainly, Ed or George or whatever your name is. This is my cat. Here are its feeding bowls. Every morning I put canned cat food into the orange bowl, pour dry food into the beige one, & water in the brown.

You never get mixed up? Put dry food in the wrong dish?

He is laughing. Sara laughs too. *Oh no. Well, not yet anyway. I suppose sometime I might try it just for fun. If I get bored or the cat does. If we feel we need a change.*

What's its name?

Name?

The cat. Doesn't it have a name?

Oh. The cat. No. Not yet. I think of it as Cat. It thinks of me as Human. Or maybe God, because of course I supply it with food & water. I have that power.

I've been looking at your books, Sara. You're quite a reader. Writers are criticized now for trying to cross borders & write from the experience of another race or gender. Do you think it's a problem? Flaubert's Madame Bovary, for instance, or Tolstoy's Anna Karenin, do you believe them? Would you know the books were written by men?

Karenina.

No. Karenin.

I'm not sure. But anyway, all of us are acting. Characters in books are actors, but we pretend to believe them. We do this with each other too.

But surely it's not that simple ...

I tell you this is my cat & you believe me. Anyway I can prove it. I can show you a cupboard full of cat food, show you the bowls: orange & beige & brown. The cat lies on my lap & purrs. The cat believes me too.

But you DO live here & own this cat. I'm not sure I follow ...

Oh, Ed or George or someone, you've developed a suave veneer. You've learned it like an actor, but underneath it you're such a child, you're so naive.

Sara sits on her friend's front porch & watches everything that happens. Neighbours toss cans & bottles into recycle boxes. Drivers cruise around & round the block searching for parking spots. Cats chase squirrels & vice versa. Maple keys spin toward the ground, weaving a soft green carpet on the sidewalk which muffles footsteps.

Sara comes & goes. There is a park at the bottom of the street & a lake at the bottom of the park. Sara walks along the boardwalk & watches waves. She begins to dream of being water.

How would it feel, she wonders, to be fluid? No restricting skin to dry out in winter, to burn in summer. No edges to bump against strangers on the subway. Nothing to define: this is Sara, all the rest is not; this is the amount of space she takes. Defending her body, this space she has always walked around in, dragging its shadow behind her like a flag.

Sometimes she feels like a stranger inside her body, babysitting it, the way she play-acts her friend's life.

Sara walks past strangers. Their shadows overlap, then move apart. She has spent so much of her life trying to dream these edges away: dissolving into union with a man, melting into him, holding him while he melts into her. Until she's no one, until her cells let go & drift apart. They float like dust motes & sparkle in the sun. They blow wherever the wind blows. But then it's over. Sara & a man put on their skin, their smiles, their clothes, & turn into whoever they were before. She practises over & over, but it always ends up the same.

The waves. Sara dreams they call to her each night.

A spider walks up the bedroom wall. Sara squashes it with a kleenex for no good reason, then watches to make sure it's really dead. It seems to be instinctive, she thinks. She sees a spider & immediately kills it. Trying to establish some balance between them, between this big space she moves inside, & those millions of small spaces spiders inhabit.

Sometimes it seems to Sara that this is the way life really is.

She sits on the back porch & counts plants in the garden: sixty-three. She tries to figure out what they are. This is harder. It is only May & few have flowers: forget-me-not, lily of the valley, the rest could be weeds. Except ferns. Except hosta. Except rhubarb. Sara is amazed she can identify so many plants. She starts on trees. She has to stretch her head up to do this, has to squint into the sun. Maple, spruce or balsam, something green, something else green, something else green.

One morning Sara opens the door to the back porch & a spider web fills the doorway. It is beautiful, in perfect concentric circles, like in a child's nature book, or a story of Little Miss Muffet. Each filament glistens in the sun. Sara sees the outside world beyond it, focused, as through a telescope. She tries to study the structure of the web in architectural terms, like a flattened-out geodesic dome, its tensile strength. If her friend had an encyclopedia Sara could study spider webs & begin to understand them.

The spider who built it is enormous; Sara kills it. So far she has killed two spiders, three mosquitoes, a sand flea, dozens of ants. Her friend who never kills anything would have carefully carried these creatures outside.

There is television here; news arrives from other countries where people keep making wars. Her friend visits another country; in a few days she'll return & expect Sara to resume her own life. Sara tries to remember it: the furniture, the pictures on the walls, the man sprawled on the bed. His spider arms reach out toward her ...

Sometimes Sara rearranges cards in the middle of the night, red cards on black on the arborite table. She does this over & over until the pattern's perfect.

•

Cockroach Dreams

•

•

THIS IS NOT A STORY ABOUT COCKROACHES. Of course not. No one would read it. People have their own cockroaches. Why would they bother to read about mine?

I want to concentrate on writing this story & forget cockroaches exist. I want to exclude them from my mind, & from my bathroom & kitchen.

There will be no real cockroaches in this story. They may crawl across the pages, but won't show up inside.

At the back corners of my kitchen shelves are small containers of poison. They look as plastic & round & innocent as children's toys, midget spaceships maybe, ready to lift off above the peanut butter if someone knew the right section to press.

At the back of one shelf is cockroach chalk from Chinatown, rumoured to be illegal. So what? Cockroaches avoid these things or have adapted. I imagine using it to chalk circles on the walls, draw cockroach outlines inside them, then slash a line across, like the no-smoking signs which invade this city like an epidemic. But I won't touch the chalk; I'm afraid to. A previous tenant bought these things. Not me. I am peaceful & love all living creatures. Anyway, thoughts of poison make me nervous.

I still dream of you at night. The cockroach dream is my favourite. It is so beautiful. We are at our best inside this dream.

We scurry together through all the dark labyrinths of this apartment, behind the books, beneath the radiator. We slip through crevices & discover the world beyond the baseboard. Becoming braver, we venture onto the vast white emptiness of the living room walls, skitter up to the ceiling & down again. Flit to & fro, delighting in the quick slim beauty of our bodies. First you lead, then I do.

What are you doing? other roaches wonder. They don't understand, aren't captivated by the drama of randomness, which for us holds such fascination.

They ask, *Why do you climb the living room wall?* We tell of the human Hillary who climbed Everest, & his answer: *Because it is there.* They shake their heads & look puzzled.

We don't care. We are blissful, in tune with each other's rhythm, perfectly, as though we've been together forever. Perhaps this is because of our sensitive antennae. The rest of the world is against us. We don't care; we have each other & don't need them.

We waken when humans fall asleep. They are noisy, even then, snoring with their mouths wide open. We skitter across their faces, dangerously close to those gaping mouths. We consider dropping inside them, the explosions that would follow, expostulations, panic, possible hypertension, stroke. This would be exciting to observe, but we're unwilling to risk being swallowed inside a snorer. Would we be able to scurry about inside one, explore interior secret passageways? We wonder about this, & think not. Anyway, their open mouths are wet & slimy. Who would want to dive inside & then be spit across the room, sticky with sputum?

We are in love with our hard dry bodies, the tiny clicking sounds we make when mating. Humans can't hear us. Our sounds are private, not like theirs. Puffs & grunts echo up & down the hallway. People in neighbouring apartments turn up radios & TVs. It doesn't matter. Human sex sounds are louder & steady & penetrate.

We watch from beneath the radiator. It is amusing. Tenants are different but the same. Tenants come & go, but we are constant.

We are quiet, you & I, private. We share a secret life. No one knows about it. We could tell them, but choose not to.

Cockroaches aren't burdened by guilt, weren't raised on some puritan pleasure-avoiding ethic, aren't trapped inside relationships of despair or apathy or habit. Cockroaches make love wherever, whenever they want to.

As humans we know this.

In the morning the fumigator will come. I signed a consent form. How could I do it?

The bathroom cabinet has been emptied of condoms & gels, toothpaste, aspirin, kaopectate. Dishes & groceries are packed into cartons & plastic bags. Nothing remains in the kitchen cupboards except toy spaceships & cockroach chalk.

Afterward, will i ever dream the cockroach dream again?

I've followed the fumigator's directions carefully, the instructions on top of my desk with letters from Greenpeace about endangered elephants, killer whales confined in aquariums, dolphin experiments. A newspaper clipping reports the slaughter of British Columbia bears, the black-marketing of their gall-bladders to the Orient. I want to save all the animals of the world except for the roaches in this apartment.

A vegetarian friend found a mouse on his pillow one morning. Now he keeps a yogurt container of poison underneath his kitchen sink. He doesn't find this inconsistent.

I weep for vanishing elephants, but turn on the bathroom light in the middle of the night & am never disappointed. There is always a roach to squash.

And you, you vanished from my waking life. One day all your belongings disappeared from this apartment. At night it doesn't matter. You linger on in these beautiful wildlife dreams:

Sometimes we lumber across a desert together. Others find our awkward humps ungainly, but we don't care. We look at each other & see only beauty.

Or: We flit from one milkweed plant to another. It's always summer. Sun shines through the orange & black stained-glass windows of our wings.

Or: We are of an ancient insect species. All the knowledge of the world is coiled inside our tight quick bodies. We will survive.

Come love, sing me your wing-click song. Listen. I sing you mine.

•

Annabel as the Universe Unfolds around Her

•

•

ANNABEL IS THE CENTRE OF THE UNIVERSE. She walks along the street & people, cars, stores, arrange themselves around her. Grass surrounds her in the park. Trees are scattered at a distance, individually, so she can appreciate each silhouette. Formal gardens are designed with her in mind: tiny alyssum first, middle-sized petunias & marigolds behind them, tall plants at the back, so she is able to view them all.

It has always been like this. Baby Annabel lay in a crib, stars & moon circling above her head. Someone moved toward her, picked her up, swaddled her in blankets, carried her from one place to another. Walls & furniture rearranged themselves around her. The warm person jiggled her up & down, crooned songs. Baby Annabel, surrounded by arms & flesh, tugged at a breast, her eyes out of focus, pale shades of shoulder, arms, face, all around her. A mass of dark hair. A voice murmuring gentle words. Baby Annabel floating inside love. She didn't know it then, of course.

Annabel walks along a sidewalk that has been placed for her convenience; houses don't crowd it, cars move alongside.

Other people walk this sidewalk too. They move closer until they're beside her, then disappear, no longer exist. Poor things. Their appearance inside Annabel's universe is so brief that she hardly pays attention, a moment later can't remember what they looked like, what they were wearing. *An old man, I think, or else a woman. I remember a blur of grey. Maybe a puppy on a leash, or was it a child held by the hand? I can't remember. After all, I can't pay attention to everything that happens.*

Of course not. But passers-by don't seem to realize this. They think they matter. They skip or hopscotch or jog or amble. They carry parcels, push shopping carts, ride bikes. They jostle into Annabel's field of vision only to disappear as she looks away to rest her weary eyes.

Because it's tiring being the centre of the universe. Annabel is conscious of her heavy responsibility. What should she do first? Walk along the shoreline so the waves can tumble toward her over & over? Stare at the sky, permitting seagulls & pigeons to fly inside it? Ride around town so the streetcars & buses won't be wasted?

She decides to read the newspaper instead. Strangers have gone to so much trouble to prepare it, to make up stories, to invent places & people & interesting events. The writers create assassinations & rebellions & famines for Annabel to read about. They think she enjoys this kind of diversion. She doesn't.

Annabel reads about the old days when scientists tried to understand how the universe worked & she smiles at their quaint theories. Thinking the earth was the centre of the universe! Imagine! Then thinking the sun was!

Annabel watches the world arrange itself around her, & wonders whether other people resent it, whether they think she doesn't deserve it. But after all, it's not her fault. She never asked for the responsibility or the honour.

People don't seem to care, never comment about it at all. They act as if they're unaware. Maybe they still believe in those old theories: earth-centred, sun-centred. People are so sweet & innocent, almost childish.

As a stranger appears inside her field of vision, Annabel smiles suddenly, a dazzling smile. The stranger's existence is so brief; it's the least she can do.

•

Football

•

•

Watch it, Arnie, says Daddy. So I watch it. Nothing happens. I don't trip over the curb. Nothing ever happens anyway, except sometimes I trip & fall. I scrape my knees. Pants get muddy. Ripped maybe.

I break things. It just happens. It happens anyway, even if Daddy says be careful. *Watch out,* says Momma, so I watch out. It doesn't matter. I bump into the table. Dishes already set out for supper. Not many break.

I bang my head on walls. They ask why, but I don't know. I just like to. It feels good. *Walking in your sleep?* asks Daddy. He is fooling. I sleep in bed.

The wall feels good against my head. They tell me, *Stop!* but it doesn't hurt. Even if it did I wouldn't cry. I'm not a baby. They make me stop so I bang the floor instead.

Doctor's office smells like medicine. *What's the matter, Arnie?* he asks. *Your folks beat you up again?* He laughs. His belly shakes. His face gets red. He asks Momma, *How about it? You push this kid around again?* They laugh. Except Momma. She looks like crying.

Doctor says if I wear a football helmet I won't get bruises on my head. *You'll be a football player, Arnie,* says doctor. *You'll wear a football helmet. All your friends will want to have one.* I guess he means Big Billy. He's the only one that likes me.

Yeah, Arnie, says Daddy. *You'll look like Dallas Cowboys on* TV.

I want to be a Dallas Cowboy. I want everyone to see me on TV.

But the helmet's too heavy. It makes me trip. It makes me do it more. I tell Momma the helmet's stupid. It bumps against the doorway. It takes up too much space.

Momma makes me wear it. Momma shows me in the mirror that I'm a football player. But I need a football. I need a football shirt with a number on the back. *Some day,* says Daddy. I ask, *What day?* He doesn't know.

Big Billy trips me with his foot. He says it's stupid to wear a football helmet without a football shirt. He asks what team I'm on. I can't remember. He asks what's my number. I don't know.

Daddy watches football on TV. He tells me teams. Dallas Cowboy. Washington Redskin. Argo. Tiger Cat. Dallas Cowboy is Daddy's favourite. I say *Dallas Cowboy, Dallas Cowboy, Dallas Cowboy.* I say it over & over, but when Big Billy asks what's my team I can't remember.

I tell him, *Dallas Redskin.* I get it wrong. It is dumb to get it wrong. Big Billy tells kids I'm a Dallas Redskin. *Laugh,* he says. *It's a joke.* The kids laugh, & I laugh.

Big Billy swats my bum. He makes me bend over like football players on TV, then swats me hard. He says real football players do it all the time. He isn't fooling. I see them on TV.

He makes me swat a bum. A lady is walking past a store. Big Billy says, *Swat her bum. She'll be surprised.*

I'm scared. I almost do it, then change my mind.

Swat the next lady, Big Billy tells me. He says I'd better do it or else he'll get real mad. I never want to make Big Billy mad.

He says, *Hurry up.* I run behind her but I'm scared to swat a grown-up. I swat her little kid instead. The kid yells. Fat lady hollers, *What the hell you think you're doing?* She walks away fast & yanks her kid.

Fat lady keeps walking fast. She yells at all the people on the street. She yells, *That kid's parents oughta watch him.* She points at me. I run after her & catch up. I grab at her too fast & bump her stomach with my head. It doesn't hurt because I wear my football helmet. Fat lady smells like perfume. She sits down on the sidewalk. I run away.

Big Billy says, *Stop crying. Football players never cry.* He's right. I see them on TV. I never see them cry.

He's got an orange. I think maybe he stole it.

He says the orange is for a football. He throws, but I can't catch it. I fall down & get all muddy.

Big Billy hides the orange under his arm, just like a football player on TV. He runs right at me. He yells at me to stop him. He knocks me over.

The orange rolls out on the street. *Hurry up & get it,* Big Billy says.

I run quick before a car drives on top & wrecks it. Cars honk their horns. I like the sound of horns.

Big Billy doesn't want the orange. It's too greasy from the street. He says it fell out of fat lady's grocery bag when she sat down on the sidewalk. He says fat lady thinks I stole it. She'll call the cops.

I'm scared. I've got to find her. I look in every store but fat lady's not inside.

I can't take an orange home. Momma & Daddy will get real mad if I've got a stolen orange.

Fat lady comes out of the bank. I yell, *Here's your orange.* I try to throw it but a lamp-post gets in the way. Fat lady walks away fast & drags her kid.

I bump into a mailbox, trip over something & fall down. *Go away,* fat lady yells. She says she'll call a cop. I throw the orange & it lands inside her grocery bag. I laugh. I never throw so good before.

Fat lady's mad. She doesn't want a filthy orange.

I run away & tell Big Billy how I gave the orange back. Big Billy can't understand me. I don't talk good. I'm out of breath. I say, *She didn't want it. But she bought it at the store. She has to have it.*

I was standing this far away, I tell him, & then I walk away to show Big Billy just how far. *Like basketball,* I say.

Big Billy says, *Wow!* He never told me *Wow!* before.

I say, *So long. I got to go.*

I throw like a basketball player, & run home fast to tell my dad.

•

Discarding

•

•

ELLIE SHAVED HER LEGS TODAY, shaved under her arms, watched her dog get put to sleep.

Lately she's been having trouble deciding which things are important. Her mind rummages through musty cartons in the basement. There are things she ought to burn, she thinks, if she only had a fireplace, things she can't leave out in boxes with the garbage for schoolkids to sort through & carry home.

Perhaps the vet will burn the dog.

Men keep asking Ellie what really happened to her marriage. They need to know this. Each weekend for a year she could tell a different truth. Each story would invalidate the ones she told before. Her ex-husband could do the same. She tells the men to be patient; one hundred truths might make the truth. But they want the short version. There is no short version.

She bought the dog after her husband, who refused to have one, walked out forever one time too often. When he came back a dog had replaced him. Perhaps he didn't even care. This time he stayed home longer. Maybe he'd always wanted her to confront him, instead of sulking, shaving her legs for him, & resenting it.

People say a dog looks like its owner & vice versa, as though they'd already seen this family & its scruffy Hungarian sheepdog.

Wait till I tie up the pup's mother, the breeder had said. *The bitch is fierce. She'll attack you*. The female was scruffy, used for breeding. *But look at the father*, the kids said. *Isn't he beautiful?* & he was, hair brushed smooth against his body, then hanging down to the ground in tight curls. Groomed for showing.

They bought the dog & never brushed it.

Hungarian sheepdogs never shed. Grass, pine needles, sand & shit became matted inside its tangled hair like an itchy blanket.

One night her husband started clipping against the dog's skin, hair by hair, releasing the mat of fur & debris above it. After ten minutes the dog was frantic so he stopped, but the next night began again. In ten minutes he could clear an area four or five inches square.

He took two weeks to clip the dog. In the meantime the creature looked awful, bald patches scattered at random as though it had mange.

Perhaps her husband thought, this is why I never wanted to have a dog. He never said it; he didn't need to. Ellie thought it for him. It was one more guilty burden for her to carry around. Her pockets were full of them.

After that she took the dog to the vet for regular clippings, where the groomer always asked, *Do you want to keep the hair? Some people do. You could weave it into an afghan or something*. Ellie always refused, wondering, could they really be serious?

Ellie took care of the dog. She fed it, cleaned up after it whenever it was sick, took it to the vet for inoculations & clipping, washed it with tomato juice whenever it tangled with a skunk. She washed the dog in tomato juice several times each year; it never learned.

She knows she did all these things, but remembering is an effort. The memory of her husband clipping the dog is much more vivid.

She wishes she could forget it, or believe it didn't matter. He trimmed the dog. So what? It's no big deal. Only ten minutes a day. Only two weeks. She wishes she could remember hearing him complain.

She'd bought the dog because every child's supposed to have one. She couldn't give the children perfect parents but she could buy them a dog.

Or to show her husband she didn't need him to come back. That she could make a life for herself & the kids after he finally disappeared. If he knew she could manage he'd be able to leave forever. Then, if he stayed home, it would have meaning.

Or, so that he'd complain & their silence would be broken.

Ellie thinks now that she bought it for all these reasons put together, as well as other reasons she hasn't figured out yet.

He couldn't complain, because then she could have said, *You weren't at home. We never knew whether you were coming back. You put all our lives on hold each time you did this. So long, kids. Don't grow up till I come back. Don't grow a quarter of an inch or I'll be sad.*

She could have said this & much more but she didn't. Unspoken conversations tangled around them. They moved carefully to avoid them. Old words needed to be clipped out of the way before anything else could be said. They both chafed & waited for the other to do something.

In old albums of snapshots the dog softens the family's rough edges. A man & woman could look at a dog & not face the camera or each other.

The dog has cancer now. It is feeble & in pain. The vet is going to put it to sleep.

All the way there she is crying. *I'm sorry, dog. I love you. Maybe*

I bought you for lots of wrong reasons, but I've loved you, & I don't even know what the right reasons would have been. Poor dog. What a burden to carry. I needed you to break us up or save us.

Later, at coffee break, Ellie can't stop talking. *Omigod, what an awful way to start the day. On the way to work I took the dog to the vet's & had it put to sleep. It had cancer.* She sips at her coffee for a moment, then says, *Dammit. I should have let my ex-husband know.*

We planned ahead when we split up. He'd come by Saturdays at noon & the kids would be waiting on the porch. One day they were playing with the dog when he arrived. The dog must have recognized the car. It bounded at the driver's side & made huge scratches on the door as it scrambled through the open window. This was a pretty big dog, you know, & there it was on top of him, & on the steering wheel, with the horn honking & the kids crying & neighbours watching, & everyone embarrassed & upset. We always kept the dog in after that.

It was hard on him leaving that dog, but he couldn't take it when he moved out. We'd bought it as a surprise when he was away. When he got home the kids were shouting, Hey Daddy! Look! We bought you something! He saw the pup, & right away he loved it. He'd always wanted one anyway.

After work Ellie goes home. She shaves her legs, shaves under her arms, even though she prefers them hairy. The shaving seems to take forever because the hair is long, but she persists. Later she wonders why.

•

Dorothy Parker Wrote the Poem

•

•

HANNAH ATTRACTS SUICIDES, the way eaves troughs attract oak leaves & cats gather fleas.

Not suicides, exactly, but those who threaten it. They tell her sad stories of their lives until she's amazed they've put it off so long. They mention the pills they've saved: pain killers from root canals & migraine, Aunt Amanda's tranquilizers, the heart pills on Grandma's dresser after she died. They study Agatha Christie mysteries & write down lethal combinations.

Patrick quotes some lines from a Dorothy Parker poem: *Gas smells awful, guns aren't lawful,* then adds. *Isn't that hilarious? She was such a genius.* But Hannah has read that poem herself & says, *Remember the last line: You might as well live? Parker was right. You might as well.*

Benny plans to polish the bathtub with Bon Ami until his naked reflection gleams. *Remember those ads, a little girl wearing a pinafore & cap? & that caption, Hasn't scratched yet? There's not much you can really count on, but Bon Ami not scratching is one of those things.* He has filled a sixty-minute cassette with a Leonard Cohen song: Suzanne will take Benny down to her place by the river; she'll do this over & over; this is the last thing that will happen to him in his life. The volume will be turned up as high as it'll go. Maybe neighbours will complain about the racket & call the cops, but it won't matter; they'll arrive too late. Benny will have already run a tub of hot water, stepped inside, & closed the sliding bathtub doors. *It will be like climbing back inside the womb,* he tells Hannah. He'll press a brand-new razor blade against his wrist, & watch layers of skin separate like a drawing in a textbook. He'll watch red blood spurt from his body. *Arterial blood does that,* he reminds her, *because it comes straight from the heart. Venous blood is darker & doesn't spurt.* Benny will float in warm pink water behind steamy frosted glass & nothing will matter, nothing will matter, nothing will matter …

Don't you mean Old Dutch? Hannah asks.

Old Dutch?

The cleanser with the little girl in a white apron, the one that hasn't scratched yet. Isn't it Old Dutch?

Benny promises to check. He won't polish the bathtub until he's sure.

Dina decided she didn't care or couldn't bear to watch the flowers grow or her children. She tells of botching her attempt, befuddled by valium & vodka. She settled back in a hot bath & slashed at her wrist a couple of times, but passed out when she saw some blood. She missed the radial artery but almost drowned. Her kids saved her but never forgave her. Dina woke up inside a psych ward. Electric shocks jolted depression from her brain & replaced it with something else: amnesia. *There are lots worse things than having a nervous breakdown,* she assures Hannah, but doesn't say what. This happened two years ago, but Dina heals with keloids, & her scars are still bright red.

Janice rings Hannah's doorbell at 5 am, barefoot & shivering. *I was this close,* she says, holding her thumb & index finger together. Hannah begins to shiver too. *Waves kept reaching toward the shore, trying to pull me in. I threw my shoes away & walked along the beach looking for the perfect spot, but then I cut my foot on a piece of glass & it was driving me crazy. Have you got a band-aid?* Hannah plugs in the kettle & spreads packets of herbal tea on the counter. Janice picks jasmine.

Marci worries that when she's ready, her husband will finally say something so sweet & loving it will tempt her to change her mind.

Hannah has nightmares every night: her friends are lined up on subway platforms, perched on the railing of the Bloor Street viaduct, standing at the brink of the Horseshoe Falls. They wait for her to save them. She loves them & it's the least she can do.

Ronnie works in a nursing home & has discovered that patients keep bottles of pills hidden in their bureau drawers. *I'm afraid I'll have to take these away,* he tells them with a look of sorrow on his face. The patients don't object. They knew they weren't allowed to have them. By now they've lost so many rights they don't complain about one more.

Sometimes Mrs Francis asks him to watch the desk a minute so she can smoke a cigarette in the bedpan room. That's when Ronnie looks up the pills in the encyclopedia at the nurses' station. He thinks about dosages all the time & has a plan, but then he meets Hannah & falls in love.

Hannah thinks Ronnie's depressed because he doesn't have her. She marries him & is sure she can make him happy. He doesn't throw out his stash of pills though. He wants to keep them like a medal to prove how strong he is, to remind him how close he came.

Hannah wishes he'd get rid of them. Whenever he's alone at home she phones him often, checking to make sure temptation doesn't suddenly overwhelm him after all.

Finally Hannah takes the pills instead. As she swallows them she thinks, at least Ronnie won't be tempted by them any more. This seems rational at the time. Later she sits around in a T-group & tries to understand.

I'm not really suicidal, she says. *I don't belong here. My friends do though. So does my husband & my sister.* The others nod in agreement. They know they don't belong in this group either.

Someone else starts to speak, but Hannah raises her voice. Now she's finally started talking she doesn't intend to stop. *This whole thing happened because of my sister. She's been threatening suicide all her life. All the way through high school she said she'd never make it to twenty-five & I believed her. I gave her whatever she wanted, my homework answers, my favourite clothes. How could I refuse?*

What happened to her? someone asks.

Hannah laughs. It sounds like crying. *She made it to twenty-six & married my boyfriend. By now she was saying she'd never make it to thirty, but she did make it, & then tried to borrow money from me as down-payment for a house. She said she needed it right away because she'd never make it to thirty-five. By then I was fed up & told her, Promises, promises. She slapped my face.*

Hannah studies the pattern on the carpet as though she needs to memorize it. *I've never forgiven myself. It was the worst sin of my life. She never spoke to me again. Maybe she still talks about dying. I've no idea. Maybe she's found people who believe her & can feel real sympathy.*

This happened years & years ago & now we're nearly fifty. We meet at funerals & weddings & don't even speak. I hope someday she'll forgive me but I know it's too much to expect.

Last night I saw a TV *show on cancer & almost checked my breasts. Isn't that stupid? Taking an overdose, then afterward checking to make sure I don't have cancer. What if a doctor told me I had only a year to live? What then? Maybe I'd phone my sister & tell her I won't make it to fifty. It would almost be worth it to hear her laugh.*

•

Myrna in the Donut Shop Again

•

•

MYRNA STICKS A FINGER in her belly to describe Arnold's incision. *They had to cut him from here to here,* she says.

Then Myrna remembers what she's wearing, her orange T-shirt & flowered pants. *What do you think of this outfit? On sale at Woolco.*

Guess how many hours he was in surgery? Seven. Guess how many days in ICU? Seven again. Isn't that amazing? I tell Arnold it's a lucky sign because seven's a magic number.

Remember ouija? I wonder whatever happened to that old board. When the kids were little we'd play monopoly & ouija every Sunday. God, remember how it was when your kids were young? Childhood seemed to go on & on forever. Days moved so slow you hardly noticed. Kids changed from one stage to another. You never knew what would happen next. I mean, you read magazine articles & Dr Spock but nothing prepared you. They described the terrible twos & you thought they must be exaggerating, but then your kid turned into a terrible two or terrible three & you could have written a book yourself.

Jody & Terry rushing home after school with crayon pictures of this & that, proud & excited. I'd guess it was a dog or cat or tree & hope I got it right. We'd tape them all over the fridge. I wish I'd kept some of those pictures, but there were so many. Every day they brought home more. I guess I thought they'd never stop. School notes. Always something I had to sign for. School trips to somewhere. I had to give permission or they couldn't go. They'd burst through the kitchen door hollering, Momma, Momma! I'd give them milk & cookies like that mother on Leave It to Beaver.

Now they live half-way across the country & phone on Sunday with nothing to say. I keep a notepad by the phone & write down things that happen so I'll have something interesting to tell. I want them to look forward to our conversations. I tell whatever I can. Euchre party. Bridge club. Someone in the church group died. But they don't care. Of course not. Why should they? I don't care what they do either, not really. I mean, I care, but it doesn't affect me. They live so far away. I don't really know their lives at all.

Arnold had so many tubes. Going in one place, coming out another. Bottles hanging on poles beside his bed. For two weeks we didn't think he'd make it. But he's okay now. He can't do much though, can't eat much either, not like he used to. Remember how Arnold loved to eat? He walks to the corner to get the paper. He watches TV. *That's it. He doesn't even bother to change the channel, just watches whatever's on, quiz shows & talk shows & the soaps.*

Isn't it amazing what they can do now? That's what I tell him when he gets depressed. They got it all. He didn't need radiation or chemo. I kid him along, tell him we wouldn't have had to watch his hair fall out. It's gone already. But it gets harder & harder to cheer him up. I tell him he's lucky, but it's like he doesn't care.

You always wanted to retire early, I reminded him this morning. A lot of guys would give their right arms to do that. Then I felt terrible. It was such a stupid thing to say. Us both thinking, how about their stomachs? Would they give their stomachs? We thought this, but didn't say it. Married all these years, & still so many things we don't know how to say.

Want another coffee? This one's on me. Maybe a donut? They keep coming up with different kinds. I joke with them about it, ask if they're trying for 57 varieties just like Heinz. The kids behind the counter look at me like I'm crazy. They're too young to remember anything.

What am I supposed to do? I can't just sit there & watch him. I come home from bowling & he's asleep. I come in from shopping or bridge club, he's lying on the sofa like a lump. Do something, I tell him. Play solitaire. Do crossword puzzles. You always wanted to read the bible from cover to cover. Why not get started?

We used to laugh when we were young. All those happy times. We had bad times too, but I can't remember them. Isn't that funny?

Maybe someday I won't remember this.

Arnold selling on the road all week, hearing new jokes. He'd tell them to me all weekend. Elephant jokes. Psychiatrist ones. We'd just keep laughing.

Nowadays I see young people laugh & I want to warn them.

This is when we're supposed to travel. All the retirement books say so. Like having a second honeymoon. Of course Arnold HAS *travelled. Did it all week for a living. But what about me? I was always home with the kids. The Golden Age Club has a bus trip to Washington. We could see cherry blossoms & the White House. Go with someone else, he tells me. Go with a woman from bowling or bridge club. But I don't want to. It's like being a widow already.*

Arnold says he can't walk far, he'd get too tired. But even if he waited inside the bus, at least he'd see some scenery that's different.

But maybe he never wanted to travel. Maybe he waited all his life to stay home, while I waited to go places & see things. We never talked about our dreams, never compared them.

I read this book once, about some woman whose life didn't get started until after her husband died. Or maybe it was a movie.

At church group when people get up to leave I start to panic. I think, oh no, please don't let it be over. Not yet. At bridge club I want to play just one more hand but the other women need to rush away. They have other things to do. They have plans.

Oh no, Doreen. Don't go yet. You've hardly said a word. Tell me what's new.

•

Alison

•

•

ALISON HAS DONE THIS all her life, lived inside bodies that are ugly, but other women live in bodies that are worse. She cannot bear to look at them. She looks away for their sake & for hers.

Her mother moves before her like an omen, her aunts, great-aunts, grandmothers.

An old woman stands on the sidewalk across the street. She wears shorts & a sleeveless T-shirt as though she doesn't care that her belly shoves them out of shape. Alison refuses to imagine the moles & scars & stretch marks on that belly. It's bad enough to see the woman's legs, awkward & veined, knobby, bowed; & the face, a collection of leather pouches, a caricature, a sculpture in plasticine by a beginner who shows no promise.

Alison never intends to look like that. She'll kill herself before it happens.

Alison used to be a child. Bump, bump, bump. Alison is small & weak & useless. Her brother sits on the carpeted staircase beside her & bumps from one step down to the next. *Try it,* he tells her. *It's lots of fun.* Alison will do anything for a big brother who pays attention. She goes bump, over the edge of one step, & thwacks her bottom on the next. She opens her mouth to cry but her brother grins, says, *Isn't that fun? Try it again!* & she does. Bump, bump, bump, down the staircase on their bottoms, shrieking with excitement, until Mother notices they are happy & makes them stop. *Stop that thumping*, says Mother. *It makes my head ache. Anyway you'll wear out the rug.* She says this as though her words have meaning to Alison & her brother, as though they care whether a carpet wears out.

Whether it disintegrates like people. Like Alison's mother who keeps a photo album on the bookshelf. On rainy days she sits at the kitchen table & stares at old snapshots while tears pour down her face. *This is me when I was your age*, she says. Alison stares at a strange child with curly hair & a frilly dress, a child whose face & hands are absolutely clean.

Spit, says Mother, & Alison spits into a handkerchief. Then Mother wipes Alison's face until it's clean enough she can stand to see it.

This is your Uncle Jordan, says mother. *You never knew him. He died before you were born. He was so much fun ...*, says this person who looks like Mother, but is crying.

Mother has a curling iron. She grabs Alison's hair & twists it tight. *Don't burn me! Don't burn me!* Alison is crying & trying to pull away. The hot tongs turn, coming closer & closer to Alison's head. Alison's hair is being curled so her picture can be taken & she'll be pretty. Years later people will look inside an album & think this curly-haired child really existed. *Now don't run around & get hot & sweaty or we'll have to do it again*, says Mother.

But Alison always forgets. Then Mother is angry & not as careful. *Keep still*, says Mother. *It's not my fault if you get burned. You won't stay still.*

Alison tries to forget she used to be that child.

Alison talks to a man. She wants to feel something, anything. His hand upon her cheek, his finger on her nipple. If he touches her she will explode into a thousand tiny pieces. She will sing & spin & dance, soar like a kite into the dazzling sky. She'll whirl away like a boomerang, then fly right back, press her cheek against the man's hand, her nipple against his finger. Away & back, away & back. She will be able to do anything. She'll turn into someone who is beautiful & perfect & spontaneous, who can skip or sing or dance, who will tumble back & forth as she feels him thump inside her. If he touches her once more it doesn't matter whether her mother said to stop that thumping. She has a nipple, he has a finger, & they touch. Alison breaks into a million zillion pieces.

Touch me, she tells the man, & she'll do anything for him, except turn on the light. *Touch me but keep the blinds down.*

An old woman waits at the foot of the bed. She is silent, like an omen, like a bad witch at a christening in some fairy tale Alison can't remember.

Alison's mother stands perfectly still. She is a lady & poses for photographs in an album. Sometimes Mother wears white gloves. She wears pearls & perfume & sends Alison to wash up. She pecks goodnight at Alison's cheek. Her long white fingers touch Alison quickly, then flick away.

Not like Alison's father who tickles her till she can't stand it. He rides her on his knees, drops her quick, then grabs her back again. He does this over & over while Alison repeats the magic rhyme that makes it happen. Alison flings her arms around his neck & hugs him. She whispers a secret in his ear, *I love you best.*

Alison's mother is putting shiny polish on her nails. *That's enough, Harley*, she tells her husband. *The child's getting too excited. We'll never get her off to sleep.*

& who could sleep? Who would want to, when a father's hands can tickle or swing her around, when he holds her in a bear hug & calls her his little princess.

Alison looks for some man like her father. *Touch me here*, she will tell him, & he will, as her body melts to honey.

Somewhere her mother frowns & smokes a cigarette. An old woman flaunts her ugliness on the sidewalk across the street. Alison won't think about that right now.

Red Riding Hood & her mother had to wait for a long time. They kept saying, *How come there's never a wolf around when you need one to eat a grandmother up?*

A man touches Alison's nipple. He nibbles. She disappears.

•

Babel

•

•

WE GO TO AMANDA'S house on Friday nights & play music & order in pizza. We still sit around & talk. But grade twelve is over & we don't talk that high school language any more. We have jobs now, & we all speak something different. It's like that tower of babel in the bible.

Danny says words like *drive shaft, Peterbilt, front-end loader*. He says *B train*. Then Gord asks, *Is there such a thing as A train?* & starts humming some ancient *Take the A Train* song, while Danny says, *Of course*, & starts explaining what's the difference. No one cares.

Cathy talks catheter, bed-pan, suction. She uses words that make us sick. She has watched a human being die.

Glenn says his mother's sick & she's scared to see a doctor. She lies on the couch all day long. Sometimes in the night he hears her crying. *What do you think is wrong with her?* he asks Cathy.

What are her symptoms? Cathy asks, & he says, *What?*

She says, *What do you notice that is different?*

Glenn gets annoyed & says, *I just told you. She lies on the living room couch all day under a blanket.*

Cathy says, *No, no. I mean symptoms. Like, does she cough? Can she eat? Are her bowels okay? Does it hurt when she pees?*

Glenn gets mad & tells Cathy it's none of her business. Does she think he & his mom talk about things like that? About her going to the bathroom? Anyway, if they did, he sure as hell wouldn't tell his friends about it.

She'd better see a doctor, Cathy says. This sounds like good advice. We look at Cathy with respect.

Peter's working in construction. He thumps on Amanda's rec room walls, testing how solid the plywood is, & how it's fastened on. He kneels down beside the baseboard & points out where nails should have been counter-sunk, if the person doing it had just taken a little more time.

Amanda gets huffy. *My dad built this room all by himself. He worked on it every weekend for one whole winter. My mother & I might hold the end of a board when he was sawing, or hold a panel in place until the nails got started, or something small like that. But my dad did all the work. He'd be exhausted from his job, but after supper he'd come down here & start to hammer anyway. I think this room looks great. Go on home & look for counter-sunk nails, whatever that means. Criticize your own parents. Leave my dad alone.*

Danny's talking about what kind of truck he likes. He says *COE*, & when someone asks him what it stands for, he acts as though he wonders who we are. *Cab-over-engine*, he tells us. *You know. Rigs where the engine is underneath the driver. The ones that are straight up & down at the front & look modern.*

Oh yeah, we all say, trying to remember what trucks look like.

Suzy says, *I thought truck engines stuck out in front, just like a car.*

That's right, says Danny. *Those are conventionals. Old-style trucks. That's what they have where I work, but I like* COES *better. They look sleek.*

Olga suggests how Suzy could change her hair. Short in the back & longer in front. She says it's the latest fashion. Everyone asks for it at the beauty shop where she works. *It would look real cute, Suzy,* she says. *I could cut it right now if you want. Hey Amanda,* she calls, *Have you got some decent scissors?*

Suzy can't imagine her hair short at the back & longer in the front. It sounds like some kind of a joke. Anyway, she's happy the way it is. *Don't you like the way my hair is now?* she asks Olga. *Don't you think it suits me?* she asks, & then regrets it.

Peter says Mr Armstrong's real sick & they've got a new teacher in to replace him. They don't think Armstrong'll be coming back. Maybe it's cancer.

Oh no! each of us is saying. *That's terrible! That's awful!* We really mean it. We try to imagine Fernwood High without old Armstrong. He's taught geography forever. He's the reason we know about tundra & delta & sedimentary rock, how come we can find countries on a map when they talk about them on the news. There's a whole world outside of Fernwood & he taught us what it's like. We think about sending him something, but don't know what. A card seems stupid. *A jigsaw puzzle,* says Amanda. No one but Amanda likes that idea. *Candy,* suggests Olga, but Cathy says it might be bad for his stomach. Finally Danny says, *How about a book?*

Everyone thinks this is a cool idea but we don't know which ones he's got. *His wife would know,* says Peter. *We could phone & ask her.* This is such an adult thing to do that it really freaks us out. No one offers to make the phone call. Maybe next Friday we'll decide something.

Amanda's ready to order the pizza. *Don't forget onions & green pepper,* Glenn reminds her. *Mushrooms,* says Olga. *Anchovies & double cheese,* Danny says. Gord asks, *Hey Danny, what's with the anchovies? You never liked anchovies before*. But it doesn't matter. Amanda ignores the anchovies anyway & orders the same pizza as always, same jumbo size, same ingredients on top.

Someone new is doing deliveries, a guy we've never seen before. *What happened to Scotty?* we ask the new guy, but he doesn't know. We don't like it when things change.

Cathy says Rick & Lydia are getting married. Her mother heard the banns read out in church. *Oh God*, says Suzy, *They're trying to act like they're grown up*.

None of us plans to get married.

Well, maybe when I'm thirty & want a baby, says Suzy.

Not till forty, says Peter. *I'll have my own construction company by then & can build my wife a house*.

Amanda says, *I don't think I'll ever get married. But if I get old & change my mind, I'll tell my husband to find something to do on Friday nights. Because I'm always going to spend them with you guys*.

Everyone says, *Hear, hear*.

Hey, says Cathy, *How do you spell that? H-E-A-R? Or H-E-R-E?*

Nobody knows, & here we'd thought old Fernwood High was perfect.

•

Asking Questions in Antiochville

•

•

PHILOSOPHERS & CHILDREN search for answers: Why are we here? Why is the grass green or the sky blue? What happens when we die?

Why do they bother? A spirit lives on or else it doesn't. Do the answers change anything that happens right now, on earth, in life? Of course not.

The uncaring planets would still circle through the heavens, measuring time & space. Worms would reduce graveyards to castings. Species evolve, then devolve to extinction. Humans murder each other & ozone & trees. Fate.

Our naked bodies were destined to meet in bed.

A thousand miles separate us. It's been two months now. I study an atlas. If we could meet each other half-way ...

I plot it with a compass & straight-edge ruler. Midway between your city & mine. A place no one has heard of. Time & the main highway bypassed it. Antiochville. I dream it into my head:

A gas pump outside the general store. Yellowed BAIT sign in the window. Angry buzz from strips of flypaper at the ceiling. A poster of a missing child thumbtacked to the wall. Cheesecake calendar beside it. Fishing tackle, plug tobacco, rat poison &

mousetraps, liniment & licorice whips. Dusty groceries, a line of black marker across each expiry date.

The volunteer fire department parks its pumper in a shed behind the store.

One church, complete with bell-tower. Signs outside, reminders of a bake sale, bingo, girl guides & brownies. Sermon for next Sunday: *What Can We Do in Antiochville to Change the World?*

A post office & flagpole. Statue of a soldier from World War I. Names inscribed on the pedestal: five Pugsley boys, the Warbriggs, Bickersleys, Blys.

Square red-brick houses with gingerbread trim. A dump truck parked in a driveway: Antiochville Sand & Gravel.

Sagging cabins beside a creek below the pulp mill. The toxic stench of frothy orange water.

We study the cabins & pick the best one.

Some windows are painted open, others shut. Bats & spiders established ownership twenty years ago. Their descendants inspect us. Twin beds, lumpy mattresses smelling of mould & generations of mice.

We could live out our lives here. Our spouses would never find us.

We'd play bingo & euchre, drink at the Legion, curl in winter. You'd wear a red & black jacket & practise pot-shots at tin cans on a fencepost until you're able to slaughter moose & deer. I'd learn to knit & crochet, swap sweater patterns. You'd slump in a rowboat at dawn & dusk, as pierced worms oozed their juices into the placid lake. I'd bake Aunt Lily's Apricot Twist Cookies & take them to bake sales, church picnics, potluck dinners. If I can find dried apricots in the general store.

Every two weeks we'd read every item in the county newspaper, catching up on all the news of Antiochville & nearby villages just like it.

If there's a library we could read books.

We'd watch game shows & sitcoms on TV. Or stare at the night-time sky & try to decide which star is which. We would stare at the stars like philosophers & ask questions: How did this happen? Why did we do this? How long will it take before love turns to hate?

The Mating Dance of the Blue-Footed Booby

RHODA WANTS TO CHECK THE WEATHER, & stands at her window hiding behind whatever clothes she wears today. Something glints at a window across the street. It is the woman with nothing to do, the woman who asked for binoculars at Christmas. She watches everyone, or only watches Rhoda. She knows everything that happens.

When a man is coming to pick her up, Rhoda waits at the front door. As his car pulls up she sprints forward, climbs in quickly, tells him to gun it.

It doesn't matter. The woman with binoculars sees everything. She nags like a guilty conscience. She knows how often Rhoda sweeps & vacuums. She monitors games of solitaire & watches out for cheating. *Too much caffeine*, she mutters, counting unwashed mugs lined up on the kitchen counter.

Today it doesn't matter; Rhoda doesn't care.

Far away the volcanic island rises smoothly from the sea. Inside the crater the blue-footed boobies are gathered. They walk back & forth on their bright webbed feet. They preen. Their feet are blue pieces of fallen sky. The boobies walk, lifting their web-shaped pieces of sky up & down, up & down, as though they're the only birds in the world that can do this. They are.

Rhoda studies her blue slouch socks. She looks up *blue* in the thesaurus to find a shade to describe them: turquoise, robin's egg, aquamarine.

Today is Rhoda's birthday & she's having lunch with Barbara. Later Eric will take her out for dinner. Perhaps he'll ask, *How about seafood?* Well, why not? Rhoda has taken the day off & her phone keeps ringing. Telemarketing calls. *Just a moment please,* then a taped message. She hangs up, but then another one calls. She imagines satellite signals bouncing back & forth in space: *Try Rhoda's phone number; she took the day off.*

Her regular telephone surveyor phones & is surprised to find her home. He asks questions about travel. *Where would she like to go?*

The Galapagos Islands.

Really? How come?

So Rhoda tells him about the boobies. Blue-footed ones are her favourites. Photos of them in flight are taped to the ceiling above her bed. *They don't look like they belong inside this world,* she tells him. *As though whoever designed them tried to be funny.* She tells of their nesting habits, the awkward way they take off & land.

The man seems fascinated. *Really?* he keeps saying.

They're so vulnerable & clumsy. Sometimes they hang themselves on bushes. Or die in an avalanche of sand from nesting too close to the edge of a crater. Even as she tells him, she wonders, can these things really be true?

He asks her to tell him more.

But, *Oh no!* Rhoda says. *Look at the time. I have to hang up. I'm meeting Barbara for lunch. It's my birthday.*

That's why you're home? You took the day off for your birthday?

Yeah. I'm going to be late. Barbara will kill me.

Of course he wishes her many happy returns. He seems reluctant to hang up. Rhoda wishes she knew his name. Maybe next time she'll ask him.

The woman with binoculars watches her hang up the phone. Rhoda wonders whether she can lip-read, & suggests an awkward place to store binoculars, but the woman doesn't follow the suggestion. Perhaps not. Rhoda waves at the pale face in the window. This is the anniversary of her birth. Nothing can annoy her.

Strangers are walking quickly along the street. They have fat or lean faces that smile or frown at random. Rhoda can't decide which combination is worse. She smiles at them anyway.

Barbara talks first. She has a new boyfriend.

Good, thinks Rhoda. Barbara needs someone. She hates doing things by herself: reading books, watching TV, listening to music.

Barbara pulls out snapshots. The boyfriend's name is Cyril. He is tall & pale & ugly. Barbara mentions that he smells like Johnson's baby powder, & now certain babies she passes on the street remind her of him. Barbara is beginning to think of babies as being not altogether unpleasant. She confides this as though it's a shameful detail, almost too intimate to mention.

Maybe he's sending subliminal messages that he wants to have a kid, Rhoda suggests. Advertising is everywhere. It's hard not to be suspicious.

It's Rhoda's turn to confide. She tells of phone surveys every night. She's pretty sure it's always the same person. She can't hang up. Perhaps it is someone who's always admired her, someone too shy to speak up. Perhaps this contact is all that keeps him going. She pictures him in his garret apartment. On his telephone with pre-programmed numbers, hers is the only one entered in. The responsibility for his life hangs heavy upon her shoulders.

Barbara laughs. Rhoda expects this.

He asked the name of her favourite TV show & couldn't believe she never watches the tube at all. *I don't have a set,* she explained. *If you don't believe me ask the woman across the street.*

When he phoned later to ask what soap she uses, Rhoda told him she'd just stepped out of the shower. They laughed. It seemed like ESP.

Does he ask about brands of talcum powder? Barbara laughs so hard she has to wipe her eyes with a paper serviette before her mascara starts to run.

Rhoda considers. *No. Never. He never asks about anything related to men or children.* Suddenly this seems significant. *But he asks about tea,* she says.

Of course, scoffs Barbara. *Tea-drinking is an easy classifier. People either drink it or don't. The tea-drinkers use herbal or regular. Regulars can be divided into those who like Earl Grey & those who don't. It's perfect. No one's left out.*

Rhoda tries to interrupt, *I told him about blue-footed boobies...*

They'll probably print the findings in the business section of the Globe, Barbara continues. *Earl Grey drinkers are the only people who read it.*

Life should be so simple, says Rhoda, & thinks it probably really is.

How is Eric? Barbara asks.

He's taking me out for dinner.

But how is he?

Well ... Rhoda wonders whether to confide in Barbara, but dammit all, why not?

Eric is taller than usual these days, or Rhoda's shorter. Sometimes, on weekends, when they're together longer than usual, their heights return to normal & Rhoda gradually remembers whatever they have in common. But usually she has to pretend. Also, Eric is beginning to sound like Rhoda's mother. When he's annoyed his voice gathers momentum. He says things like, *Kemmely dudsn dqhgapt zyo yeowntp wnytohewo?* & EOJMYOUETHE!

Rhoda can't ignore his voice although she has no idea what he's saying. His side of the conversation sounds so unpleasant. Her side is silent.

Do you love him? Barbara asks. The eternal question.

Love, Rhoda wonders. What is it? *I'm breaking up with him this evening.* Rhoda makes the decision as she speaks. *I'll have do it quick, before a gift.*

She could tell him in her own flat but the woman with binoculars would unnerve her. Anyway restaurants are neutral places. No one hollers or throws dishes or causes bruises & black eyes. She will tell him quickly & go home. She'll be shivering. Her boots will squeak in the crisp snow. When she gets home she'll make a cup of herbal tea to warm up. While the kettle boils she'll measure the living-room window. Tomorrow she'll buy a blind on her lunch-hour. Of course. She should have done this long ago.

Perhaps the telephone survey man will call. It is her birthday after all. He'll want to ask about her day & learn more about blue-footed boobies.

In the Galapagos Islands sun is beginning to melt through the mist. Leaves stir. Giant tortoises walk slowly, with dignity, aware of the magic of their existence.

A male booby whistles. His wings lift. His head & tail point toward the early morning sky. His bright blue feet move slowly up & down.

There is a rhythm inside her. She almost remembers it. The sky is empty. She points toward it. Her feet are pieces of blue sky. She moves them faster. Dancing against the hot volcanic sand. Dancing. Dancing.

•

Emily Moving On

•

•

I'm one of the Dionne quintuplets. Emily tells this to strangers in a Vancouver coffee shop or on a park bench or in a bus. *Remember us? The freak show of the thirties. We were born in Ontario. In Corbeil, near North Bay.*

People stare in amazement. *Wasn't it Callander?* someone asks.

Corbeil. A lot of people make that mistake. Tourists drove for miles to watch us play. Neighbours sold souvenirs & hot dogs & gasoline. The gas station had five pumps. People would ask for a fill-up from the one with their favourite quintuplet name.

Someone says, *It's hard to imagine ...,* but Emily's still talking.

... a barrel of free rocks beside the gate labelled FERTILITY STONES. *Couples took them home to put under the mattress. If the wife got pregnant they knew the stones worked. We advertised Quaker Oats, Karo Syrup, Palmolive Soap ...*

Which quint are you? someone asks, & she says, *The one with epilepsy. The one who died.*

Dammit, she thinks later, turning this way & that, bedding twisted in a knot. Why did I say all that? It's Kenny's fault. I need him back. Then she thinks of a picket fence, white pointed staves around a fortress. Someone tries to escape, is impaled on top. It looks like Emily. She changes her mind.

Or: *I'm a poet,* she admits shyly.

Really! Strangers stare in amazement, as though they never dreamed they'd ever meet one. *Has your work been published? Would I recognize your name?*

Emily Dickinson, she says, & begins to recite:
  The Trees like Tassels – hit – and swung –

People drift away but Emily keeps on reciting anyway:
  There seemed to rise a Tune...

Now she moves from Vancouver to Victoria. *Because of Emily Carr?* people at work ask her. *Maybe,* she tells them. They are joking; she is serious. *I'm named after her, you know,* she says, as though her parents had ever looked at paintings, ever known the names of people who made them. *I'm moving to James Bay, the old neighbourhood where she used to live.*

Emily once travelled to the other James Bay, at the south end of Hudson Bay. She was searching for something then too. She boarded the Ontario Northland Railway, rode north through scrubland to Moosonee, travelled by kayak to Moose Factory on the island. She walked in the footsteps of Indians, traders, explorers, pretending she was Cree. When was that? she wonders now. Long ago; she knows that much. Before Kenny.

Now she criss-crosses Vancouver, goodbye this place, goodbye that. She walks the shore of English Bay. Where do the ships go when they leave here? she wonders once again. She munches a last muffin in her favourite coffee shop, checks the sale table at the library, withdraws twenty bucks from the 7-11 bank machine for old-times' sake. Goodbye goodbye.

It is fall. Hydrangea bushes on Barclay Street fade, their blossoms desiccate, become more delicate each day. Emily holds her camera too close, so the flowers will be out of focus, an impressionist blur of colour. Good.

Lost Lagoon, the crisp white swans, greedy Canada geese. Other birds with names she always meant to learn. Emily stares up at each totem pole in Stanley Park: *Goodbye. Goodbye.* She doesn't think about the Indians, their spirit creatures; she thinks of Carr in the Queen Charlottes, painting totem poles, quick, before they're gone.

She visits the Vancouver Art Gallery one last time, the Carr posters & postcards in the gift shop. Finally up the escalator to the gallery, & there they are. How could Kenny have ever mattered? Her mind ignores him, like tree-tops. Good-bye *Mountain Forest* & *Tree Trunk* & *The Little Pine.* Goodbye *Scorned as Timber, Beloved of the Sky.* Finally her favourite, the hardest to leave: *A Young Tree.* The green heart of the tree tries to curl around her, pull her inside. This is the first time she's actually cried.

In the coffee shop Emily passes by the shiny cakes & pies & brownies, as always, but then thinks, why not? She considers cheesecake & butter tarts, finally decides on blueberry pie. *I grew up on a reservation in Ontario,* she tells the young man who takes her money. *We picked blueberries in the bush & sold them to folks in town.*

He stares. *You don't look Indian,* he says. *You've got black hair but ...*

Cree, she assures him. *Mosquitoes! Clouds of them. We were covered in bites.*

Emily studies the coffee urns: Regular, Decaf, Special Blend. This day IS special; she picks the third one.

Finally she's ready to move across the water to Victoria. She stands at the front of the ferry, to see where she's going, not where she's been.

In James Bay history surrounds her: the big frame house where Carr grew up, her *House of All Sorts*, the house she lived in later with her blind sister. At night mist drifts past the window. Emily lies in bed & sees a cloud shaped like Carr's ghost, a parrot perched on her shoulder. She pushes an old baby carriage with a monkey inside it. Emily opens the window wide & hollers, *You lived without a man. How did you do it?*

She explores up one street & down another.

The Carr house is painted creamy yellow & has a historic plaque out front. Emily Carr was born here in 1871. Volunteers in old-fashioned dresses can point out this & that to tourists. The house is open from June to September. Luckily it's now October. Emily won't meet straggles of chattering tourists. Intruders. Emily's doesn't feel like an intruder herself. Of course not. She lives here now.

Emily stands by the picket fence, reads the historic plaque. Words. Only words. Where is the hawthorn hedge for three little girls to hide behind? The cow barn with its loft studio? Where is the square red & white ambling cow? Where are mother & father, older sisters, little Dick? The three little girls in starched white dresses with pinafores on top, who clutch at lop-ear rabbits with button eyes, who play at being grown-up ladies behind the hawthorn hedge. Those three little girls: Big, Middle, Small, where are they? Two little girls stayed clean & neat. The other, the youngest, into mischief, her pinafore stained from animals & dirt & life ...

She & Kenny could have made babies. She'd have lived surrounded by children. Maybe one would grow up & live out her mother's dreams. As if Emily even knows what her dreams are, as if she's figured out anything. Mothering children might have given her life meaning. Women used to think so. That's what Kenny wanted. Why couldn't she have wanted it too?

Emily lurks late at night outside the apartment house on Simcoe Street, *The House of All Sorts*, built in the old cow pasture. The lights are out, so she can imagine the inside the way she wants: chairs hoisted by pulleys to the studio ceiling to create space. Paintings, spirit talk, on the walls. The coffin-box of sketches, with brushes & turpentine on top. The first northern light of morning would draw her eyes up, up the little staircase to the attic bedroom. Two giant totem eagles hover, their heads toward the roof peak, their outstretched wings covering the ceiling. A few feet below them someone sleeps.

In the dark back garden, the cherry tree with its monkey-box for Woo. Apple trees, lilacs, wall-flowers, sweet alyssum. Beyond, in the kennels, Punk, Loo, Adam, Flirt, all those restless bobtail sheepdogs await their morning run in Beacon Hill Park.

Emily listens for the sounds of bobtails, monkey, white rat, Persian cat, creaking stair treads, fractious tenants, bawling babies. Silence. Only silence.

An ordinary family must live inside. Children roll marbles across the slanted floors. *What are these for?* they ask their parents, yanking at pulleys. *We've got to get rid of these old things,* the parents remind each other.

Every day Emily tramps about the neighbourhood & imagines Carr talking beside her. *It was better in the old days, before sidewalks, before the streets were paved.* Emily nods. Everything was better then. Of course.

Emily wanders through Beacon Hill Park. A couple embraces beneath the trees as though no one is nearby. Emily backs away quietly, but it doesn't matter; no one else exists inside their world.

A pang of memory: Kenny lies beside Emily in Stanley Park & strokes her belly. *It's so soft,* he tells her. Emily knows all bellies are soft. Kenny makes the nice generic comment he's already made to other women. How many? Why does it matter? Right now he says the words to her & they work. Her legs melt apart, he fits inside her. *Nice,* he says. *Nice,* a word he always uses, a word other women would recognize too. Emily knows this, but the words work anyway.

A couple do the same thing in Beacon Hill Park. Everywhere people make love & pretend nothing will change. How do they do it? she wonders. Maybe love helps.

Emily explores streets, one after another. Carr would have seen these same houses, known the people who lived inside. So what?

Each house is different. If she lived in the mauve stucco with dark wood trim, would her life be different than it is now? Of course. What about the grey frame with the circular porch? A different life again. As if there are all these other lives possible, waiting for her to toss a die & decide.

Mr Carr's building on Wharf Street has been turned into a gallery. Paintings & photographs hang on the walls. What does it matter? What does any of it matter? Carr is lost; Emily can't find her. Emily is lost; she can't find herself either.

She visits a grave, reaching out, looking for something, but doesn't know what. Soul, maybe, she thinks, then laughs at how ridiculous she is.

She decides to visit the trees. *Art is art,* Carr wrote, *nature is nature. You cannot improve upon it.* Emily takes one bus & then another to reach Cathedral Grove. She sees the trees Carr painted. Their trunks only, like ruins of Greek temples, columns designed by an architect in order to support the sky. Emily looks around, holds her breath. Yes. A ghost paints at an easel. She wears a long skirt & rubber boots. A monkey cavorts around her feet.

The tree-tops are far above, tangling the clouds, scraping against the sky.

Emily wanders through spaces between trees. She stares at ancient Douglas firs, survivors of the twelfth century. People are insignificant beside them, their tiny problems & life-spans, silly feelings of importance. The trees simply endure, Emily thinks. They stand here & wait to die, as we all do. Meanwhile they support the sky, linking earth & sky together.

Emily touches the dappled ground, the ferns & tree trunks around her. Life surges. Green changes from one shade to another. Photosynthesis is taking place. The forest is moving, curving. Spaces open between the trees so Emily is able to enter. She feels how tree trunks & greenery turn in slow motion, unwind, then pull her inside.

Emily remembers the painting in the Vancouver gallery: *A Young Tree, 1931*. Carr painted the tree's green heart, the essence of treeness, essence of life. Emily stands very still, her feet rooted to the earth, gathering strength from far beneath the forest floor. She reaches upward, farther & farther, until her branches embrace the swirling sky. The sky is whirling, earth turning ...

In 1931 Carr travelled inside a tree, & now Emily makes that journey too.

•

Heartbreak Is the Name of a Hotel

•

•

CORINNE AVOIDS ROMANCE NOVELS. All the same, hearts are everywhere. They surround her in this used bookstore like red cut-outs in a kindergarten on February 14th.

She flips through pages of an old recipe book. *Heart Pie: Follow directions for steak & kidney pie, substitute cooked heart.* Someone said the way to a man's heart is through his stomach, she remembers. Obviously not the author of this book. *Stuffed Heart: Steam heart, pack with crumb stuffing, brown in oven. Heart Fingers: Cut heart into fingers, dip in milk, dredge with flour, proceed as with any other fingers.*

Eat your heart out, Corinne thinks, & then wonders, didn't some Indian tribe eat the hearts of brave enemies in order to obtain their courage? *Cor-age.*

The yellowed pages crumble between her fingers. Is this recipe book valuable? Corinne hopes not. She replaces it on a shelf & picks up another book, anything, a distraction.

An anatomy text. Someone underlined a quote from William Harvey. Her friend Marni is a nurse & probably has textbooks praising Harvey for figuring out blood circulation. Did other scientists & the church believe him? In the 1600s? Probably not.

Corinne's heart contracts, she feels it happen. Blood surges from her right ventricle toward her lungs. A valve prevents the blood from falling back.

Do you love me? she'd asked, needing to hear it, but not this way, because if he said yes after being asked it wouldn't count. Anyway he didn't say it.

Blood flows back into her left atrium. It has been gathering oxygen. She is supposed to feel refreshed.

She remembers a line from a poem. Was it by Donne? *The day breaks not; it is my heart.*

Heartbreak is the name of a hotel. You stay awhile but then move on. She needs to believe this.

Hearts are found in strange locations. She considers them: on one's sleeve, in one's mouth, in the highlands, in San Francisco, buried at Wounded Knee, in the right place. Hearts move though: sometimes go out to someone, stand still, leap up, run away with one's head, like the dish runs away with the spoon.

Nursery rhymes tell something; it's hard to know what: *The Queen of Hearts, she made some tarts, all on a summer's day. The Knave of Hearts, he stole the tarts & took them clean away.*

How are you? she should have asked him instead, her tone cordial, meaning: hearty, sincere, warm.

Coronary, from corona: encircling like a crown. He is dead now. It shouldn't matter.

Do you love me? she'd asked, & he answered, *What is love?*

Her left ventricle contracts; an electrical impulse causes this to happen. Blood circulates around her body, warms her extremities: *cold hands, warm heart.*

The woman phoned her. The *other* woman ...

Corinne leaves the bookstore, goes to the supermarket to find food for supper. Slabs of shiny red muscle glisten in a refrigerated display case, knives lined up on the wall behind them like dissection instruments. Corinne feels like throwing up. She is turning into a vegetarian.

Richard. *It means Lion-hearted,* he used to tell her. *Coeur de Lion.*

O Richard, how could you die? How could you leave me? she asks over & over, knowing he'd already left her long before.

The woman had phoned her in a panic, wasting precious time; she should have been dialing 911. *Something's wrong with Richard!* she'd shouted, & then, *You don't know me. Something's the matter. You'd better come over ...* Then she'd hung up, forgetting to tell Corinne the address.

Soft-hearted, hard-hearted. Hearts are made of iron, steel, oak. Othello: *My heart is turned to stone; I strike it, and it hurts my hand.*

Robert Louis Stevenson loved wholeheartedly: *The friendly cow all red and white I love with all my heart: She gives me cream with all her might, To eat with apple tart.* It is riskier to love people. Anyway, is that all there is to it? Give me what I want & I'll love you back. Is it that selfish? That simple?

Corinne wonders now, did she really love him wholeheartedly, asking herself as he did: *& what is love?*

He gave her something she didn't want. Memories. Too bad. He's not dead as long as she remembers. Absence makes the heart grow fonder. Damn.

All the same, the sun shines in the funeral parlour window, blood enters her right atrium, the circulation cycle continues to happen.

Her friend Marni is down from Parry Sound for the funeral. *He was a shit, Corinne,* Marni says. *Everyone knew it. We thought you knew it too.*

Something happened on my holidays, Marni continues. *It was weird.* She tells of standing on the shore of Georgian Bay early in the morning & watching Indians paddle toward her. *Old-time ones,* she says, *like in a movie about voyageurs. Mist was lifting from the water. The canoes glided closer & closer. They almost reached me, then disappeared, simply dissolved inside the mist. I stood on solid rock,* Marni says, *but it was as though the ground was moving. Later I saw a red salamander. I've been going there since I was a kid & never saw a red one before.* Marni waits for some appropriate response, but then continues, *Then on TV that night I heard about an earthquake in Mexico, & suddenly it all made sense.*

Is she crazy? Corinne wonders. Does she think the salamander travelled all the way from Mexico to Canada through some fissure inside the earth? Of course not. But she believes these things are signs, & happen so we can see them & try to understand.

He came on to me once too, Marni says.

Corinne thinks of fault lines, inside hearts, inside the earth. Hearts get damaged. Richard's stopped. Hers is already beginning to mend. But a salamander is the colour of arterial blood & wanders lost near Georgian Bay.

•

Turtles

•

•

THE PHOTO HANGS ABOVE JENNIFER'S DESK: a turtle emerges from its shell & awkwardly clambers toward fresh water. This happens in 1994 or a hundred million years ago. After all, what does time mean to a turtle? What does time mean to anyone?

Time moves forward & backward, like memory, like videotape. A woman fiddles with a rewind button, & gets angry with the picture she finds; she fast-forwards & rewinds until she finds some other time.

* * *

A grandfather clock stands in a hallway. A table in the corner has a crocheted runner on top. On top of the runner are several copies of *National Geographic*. A child sits on a small oriental carpet & faces the clock. She holds a magazine open at shiny pictures of turtles.

Giant clock guards the hallway. Grandfather is what Jenny's mother calls it. Grandfather is bigger than everyone, especially Jenny, who recites the hickory dickory verse & hopes this will make the clock feel happy. Perhaps if it is happy then the tick tick noise will stop.

Jenny recites the hickory words & imagines Mickey Mouse & Minnie playing in the hall. Mickey & Minnie wear cute little clothes & run up & down the clock. Sometimes they bring their Pluto dog. Jenny likes them.

The clock has long gold sticks with big gold circles. Jenny watches through the glass & sees them swinging back & forth. They never stop. *Watch them anyway,* says Mother. *Don't bother me until they stop.*

Jenny hears her mother making noises & the man makes noises too. The sounds are quiet & far away because the bedroom door is shut.

Jenny sits on the hall carpet & watches the gold circles move back & forth. When big girls skip double dutch on the sidewalk, their feet move like that but fast. Jenny wants to be big. She wants to skip with dancing feet & never trip.

Jenny is quiet. Only her mother & the man are allowed to make any noise.

Jenny knows her mother isn't crying because one time she was very bad & went upstairs to see. *Never never never!* yelled Mother. *Never never!* yelled the man. Then Mother spanked her with a ruler.

Jenny doesn't think the clock will stop. Mrs Jeffers owns this house & everything inside it. Mrs Jeffers winds the clock every morning with a key. Jenny knows the place in the hall closet where the key hangs on a nail.

Be a good girl, says Mother. *Watch the clock so you can tell me if it stops,* So Jenny watches. Maybe this only happens once in a while: Mrs Jeffers goes to church group & a man comes to visit & Jenny gets to watch the giant clock.

Jenny's afraid to look away in case she doesn't notice the stopping happen. Jenny can look at Mrs Jeffers' magazines if she is very careful turning pages. This time the magazine has turtle pictures.

One day Mrs Jeffers told Jenny a story about a rabbit & a turtle. Jenny thought it would be fun to be a rabbit that could hop & hop & hop. Mrs Jeffers said the story means it is better to be a turtle.

Jenny tries to be quiet like a turtle. Turtles can stay still for a long time. Jenny looks at magazine pictures & tries to understand how they do it.

Oh for heaven's sake stay still, says Mother. *Don't fidget. Keep quiet. Little children should be seen & not heard.*

The grandfather clock has long gold sticks with gold circles at the bottom. They move always, but are quiet. Somewhere inside the clock is a tick tick sound that never stops. There are other gold sticks up at the top. *Hands,* says Mother. *They aren't sticks, Jenny. Call them hands.*

Jenny has hands. She wiggles fingers that look like sticks.

When the clock hands are in one of the magic places the clock makes music. No one minds if the clock makes lots of noise. Jenny can be noisy at the same time & no one will notice. She can say anything she wants, even bad words.

Other times Mother would wash the bad words from her mouth with soap until she's sick. *Where do you hear this stuff?* asks Mother. Jenny tries to tell but it's too late. Mother is already putting soapsuds in her mouth.

The tick tick sound is very loud & Jenny watches the gold circles that never stop. The hands are in a magic place & the music starts to play & Mrs Jeffers comes back early like a surprise.

What are you doing? asks Mrs Jeffers & Jenny tells how to watch the gold circles until they stop.

Mrs Jeffers has cookies inside a tin. Jenny can eat them. Jenny & Mrs Jeffers look at turtle pictures in the magazine.

A turtle climbs out of an egg. There are no other turtles in sight. *Where's its mother?* Jenny asks. Mrs Jeffers says mother turtles lay their eggs, then go away & don't come back.

This happens, even though turtles are very quiet & never fidget.

•

Short Stories

•

•

ELLEN WEARS NO MAKE-UP THIS MORNING, no watch or jewellery. She has five dollars in her wallet. She takes a paper from her pocket & rereads the instructions. *I'm just for short-term admission,* she tells the receptionist, meaning, I'm not like these others.

She looks around the waiting room & feels sorry for the other patients. Did they hear her? Are they jealous? Do they know what short-term admission means? Admitted in the morning, surgery in the afternoon, back home again the same evening. The others look like they will stay inside these hospital walls until they die.

The woman crosses Ellen's name off a list & says, *Wait over there until we call you.* So Ellen sits with old grey people who wear no make-up or watches or jewellery. They stare at empty walls or leaf through tattered magazines.

Ellen has brought a book to read. A librarian had recommended the short story collection, saying, *What? You don't know this author? I thought English teachers read all the latest fiction*, as though, what kind of teacher could Ellen possibly be? What kind of person?

Have you read all the books in your library yet? Ellen wanted to ask.

A clerk calls people to a desk & asks questions. Ellen tries not to listen to their private information.

The book is called, *What We Talk About When We Talk About Love*. Ellen thinks the title must be ironic, because of course people don't talk about love at all. It's too personal. Anyway they shouldn't need to. Ellen has told men she loves them. She told a husband when she had one, & other men before & since. Men said the same thing back. But they didn't talk back & forth about it, what she meant & what he meant. Explaining would have spoiled it. Ellen thinks this whenever she glances at the title.

Her children know she loves them. She told them when they were young. They're in their teens now, & she can't say the words any more. She'd feel awkward & so would they.

A man's wife is having a caesarean section & he can't remember the name of her doctor. The clerk asks his wife's name but it doesn't show up on the computer. The man spells it over & over as though repetition will make a difference. A supervisor tries to help. Finally they realize he has given his wife's first name, not her last one. Ellen thinks maybe the author could write about this & make it believable. The people in the book seem much more real than the ones inside this room.

The person beside her sighs. Ellen glances at her quickly, then looks away. The girl seems far too young to be here. *I'm glad it's cloudy*, the girl says. *It'd be even worse if the weather outside was nice.*

Ellen smiles politely, then returns to her book: Two couples are at a bingo game, a young couple & a retired one. The young people laugh a lot & touch. They ignore everyone else. The older man is sure they're cheating. His wife comes back from the bathroom & is silent, then tells him she's spotting again. *This is what life is really like*, he wants to tell the young couple. *This is what happens next.*

Ellen thinks he's right. This is what she could warn the young girl who sits beside her, what she could tell her son & daughter. They think everything's easy. They take good health & love for granted.

Perhaps the gynaecologist will find out she's all right. Perhaps her heavy bleeding has no meaning.

Ellen & her daughter sometimes joke about their periods. They say if men had heavy bleeding they'd brag that it was macho. This isn't original; they read it in a book by Gloria Steinem & laughed & laughed. Then the daughter read it to her brother, who didn't find it funny. *Men are like that*, Ellen had said.

She'd told them she had to have a D & C but didn't mention the biopsy; they could figure it out for themselves. After all, young people know everything these days. They learn it all in school. They know about contraception & anatomy & sex-diseases before they're in their teens. Parents never need to mention sex at all.

They hadn't understood. She'd overheard her daughter, *Probably it's pretty common. Probably all women have to have this when they're old*. Ellen had wanted to interrupt, *I'm only forty-two*, but knew they wouldn't find this a contradiction.

Ellen looks at the people lined up on benches. She tries to decide which ones are old & which ones aren't. Her mother's age is old. Her own age isn't young, but it's certainly not old. Middle age is such a middling term for it.

Her children think she's old. It's only fair; Ellen always thought her mother was too. Did her mother resent it when she was younger? Her mother's almost seventy now. Does she think she's old yet? When did she start? Suddenly Ellen needs to know.

Just one more D & C before I stop for a coffee, the clerk mutters under her breath. Ellen listens & thinks, good, I must be next, but they call the young girl beside her, who looks younger than Ellen's daughter.

Ellen tries to imagine having an abortion. She wanted both her kids. Sometimes she thinks she got married just to have them. But if she'd been young, unmarried, in high school? Could she have carried a child nine months? Everyone whispering & staring as her belly got bigger & bigger. & then what? Could she have kept it? Of course not. Unwed mothers didn't in those days. Could she have faced giving it up? She doesn't know. She knows grammar, not things that matter.

Love-children, her mother always called them, as if babies born in wedlock weren't. Ellen wonders where it happened. The backseat of a car? A neighbour's couch while babysitting? Sudden passion. No time for contraception. No thought of it.

Ellen wonders whether her daughter is on the pill.

Or perhaps they made love outside. A park or field. A backyard. The rustling of leaves, & of small animals mating around them.

The young girl has disappeared, must have already been taken upstairs.

Ellen wants to phone her children & make sure they haven't grown up while she's been in here. Her daughter could be getting pregnant at this moment; her son could be fathering a child. There are things she should have told them when they were younger & easier to talk to. Things she still could tell them if she knew which words to say. She could call them from a pay phone before they leave for school, could say, *I love you,* then hang up quick. They'd think she was crazy.

She reads the title story instead. Two couples talk of love, how it made someone crazy, how it's different for different people, & what happens when it's over.

Where did it go? Ellen wonders. How could she love someone & then stop? Feel an empty place inside her when she hears about him later. Love: now you feel it, now you don't. Was it ever love in the first place if this could happen? The feeling for her kids is different. Natural, unforced, permanent. Ellen never wonders whether she loves them; she just does.

There ought to be different words for all the different kinds of love, she thinks. Someone should make up some.

At the end of the story one of the women says, *Now what?* Ellen thinks she could be the person talking. She'll have her D & C, then later find out the results. But even if the biopsy is normal, if everything seems just the same as always, now what? she'll be wondering, now what?

•

Maude

•

•

Remember ...? says Maude, & then she stops. Everyone tries to remember. She is telling stories about the old days. Or trying to. Children & grandchildren are gathered round.

Was it about Christmas? asks her son Charlie, because someone had mentioned winter. Maude shakes her head. *About Thanksgiving?* She shakes again. *About the house? The dog? Was it about Papa?*

Maude grits her false teeth together as though she'd like to bite whoever's talking. Is it Charlie? It sounds a little like him, but not exactly. *Who are you anyway?* she asks him, but no one answers. The teeth-grinding always makes Charlie nervous. He is behind the kitchen door drinking scotch straight from the bottle so no one will find a glass & know.

Charlie's sister Lucille takes over. She stays calm. *Listen, Momma, I'm going to list everyone in the family. Tell me when I get to the person you're trying to tell about. Okay? I'm going to get started then. Here I go. Now remember, I'm listing everyone in the family, so it may take me a while to get to the one you want. Just be patient until I get there. Okay? Here goes then. Charlie? Me? You know me. I'm Lucille. Not me? How about Glenna then? Or maybe Boyd. Don't forget now. You're supposed to stop me when I get to whoever you were trying to talk about.*

Maude has forgotten. If she ever knew what she wanted to say she has forgotten. She has no idea what Lucille is doing. She has forgotten everything except how much she dislikes Lucille. Maude would like to be the one who could remember & think of words. She would like Lucille to stumble & get confused. She would like to talk to Lucille the way Lucille talks to her, as though she's only two years old. Slowly. Distinctly. Too loud. She glares at Lucille. She grinds her teeth. But Lucille doesn't notice & get scared. Maude tries to look fierce. She screws her face up.

Lucille notices & hugs her. *Don't cry, Momma. It doesn't matter. You'll remember about it later.*

There is a baby in this room. It wears purple striped pyjamas. Maude remembers layettes, flannelette nightgowns with rows of smocking along the top, bonnets with ribbon rosettes, booties with pompoms, special baby wool with a silver thread. This baby wears striped pyjamas like someone's husband. Or a baby dressed up as a convict for Hallowe'en.

Someone wants her to hold this baby so he can take a snapshot. *Blanket,* says Maude, meaning, put a blanket around this baby so he won't look like someone's husband wearing striped pyjamas, so he won't look stupid in this picture.

She's cold, says some woman Maude has seen before. Charlie's wife maybe, whatever her name is. Or maybe Maude's other daughter. Doesn't she have another daughter? She isn't sure.

It's because of all this noise & confusion. All these people. Sometimes her thoughts make perfect sense. Sometimes she sits in her rocking chair & remembers anything she wants. She even remembers things she doesn't want to.

Lucille is saying names, as though she has some reason to do this. Lucille used to be two years old. Maude used to be clever & could keep her in her place. In her playpen or in her bed. Maude could decide whether to pick her up or not, whether to pretend she couldn't hear her. She wishes now that she'd let Lucille cry for an hour before picking her up.

Because she would have been all right. Alive & kicking, & breathing. Breathing, that was the main thing. The main bad thing that happened to babies was that they turned blue & dead for no reason. Even the doctors could not explain it. This is the thing that Maude had worried about all the time. She never let her babies cry. They were her whole life then. Sometimes she deliberately banged around so they'd wake up. She'd stare at them while they were asleep & be amazed that they were hers.

Some woman is listing names of people & looking at Maude as though Maude knows why in the world she does this. *Oh, for heaven's sake, shut up*, says Maude, who wants some peace. Surely at her age she is entitled.

•

Mothers: Why Won't They Tell Us the Meaning of Life?

•

•

THE STREETCAR IS CROWDED OF COURSE. It's always rush hour when I travel; I'm always standing, but sitting can be worse.

Beside me two fresh-faced teenage boys ask a stranger what he thinks is the meaning of life. This happens without preamble. The man is trapped in an aisle seat & the boys loom above him. They seem to ask the question sincerely, as though he must have figured it out by now & will surely be glad to tell them.

I figure it must be some kind of joke, & am glad to be distracted from the memory of meeting Kate for lunch. But I begin to inch away from the boys for fear they'll ask me next. Other passengers do this too, & soon a little space is created around them.

So what do you think? the boys persist.

You're not asking me at a very good time, the man says. I study the man & wonder why this time is worse than any other. Has he just lost his job? Broken up with a lover? Buried a family pet? Had a confrontation with his mother? Or is it only women who have trouble with mothers? This reminds me of Kate again.

I'm tired out, the man says. *On my way home from work. I haven't had supper.*

Oh yeah. Maybe after you've kicked your shoes off, read the paper, turned on the TV ...

That's right, he says. *I'll be relaxed then. I'd be able to seriously consider the subject.*

So maybe that's what the meaning of life is to you. Relaxing, drinking a couple of beers, watching a hockey game or talk show...

The man smiles. *A Molson would be good right now.* I can tell he means it.

One of the boys isn't crazy about this answer. *Yeah, but when you watch the six o'clock news ...* he begins, but the other boy interrupts. *Leave the guy alone, Jerry. He gave us his answer. He told us what he thinks is the meaning of life.*

I stare at the man, wondering whether he has any extra bits of wisdom he wants to add, but he is silent. Apparently not. He gets up & brushes past them, muttering. *Excuse me. This is my stop.* I doubt it. I imagine him waiting on that bleak corner for another crowded streetcar. He won't get a seat on the next one. On the other hand, standing up makes it easy to move away from pestering strangers.

I think about *The Hitchhiker's Guide to the Galaxy* where people search for the meaning of life & finally discover it's a number, seventy-two or twenty-six or something. I know the boys would love that book, but I decide not to tell them about it. They'll have to figure out the meaning of life for themselves, like everyone else. Anyway, it's probably different for everyone.

The boys keep talking. *I guess it's kind of threatening, having people ask such a heavy question.*

Yeah. But how else are we going to find out?

If that had been your dad what would he have said?

Computer games. He disappears into the den after supper & we never see him again. What about yours?

I haven't seen him since nursery school.

Parents don't tell the things that matter. They talk steadily though, so their children won't notice. We all were kids once; we have complaints.

At lunch Kate complained about her mother & no wonder. Her mother had called her by someone else's name, someone Kate had never heard of: Martha. Kate grumbled, *Why do I bother to visit her anyway? That little old grey-haired stranger isn't my mother. My mother had all her marbles.*

Who is Martha? Kate had asked her mother, but the answer wasn't reassuring: *My daughter. My daughter Martha.*

Martha? Kate's an only child. Or is she? Did Kate have an older sister who died before she was born? Or was stillborn? Put up for adoption? Questions tumbled through Kate's mind, & she started to ask them, but suddenly her mother fumbled for her nitroglycerine pills, popped one into her mouth & spilled the rest on the carpet. By the time Kate retrieved the pills & replaced them in the container, the moment was gone.

Mothers know how to distract us. They started when we were toddlers.

Next time I visit, Kate told me, *I'm going to do the same thing back. I'll call her Harriet or Aunt Myrtle. I've always hated both those names.*

Good idea, I encouraged her. *Score one for us daughters.*

We all have mothers, of course. They taught us things indiscriminately, as though they were all of equal importance: *Don't turn back the corners of pages. Say your prayers. Do unto others... Soak dish towels in bleach.* It's up to the kid to figure out which words are more important. We all have complaints; Kate didn't give me a chance to talk about mine.

Another thing, Kate added, *she never washes her comb any more. There's all this gunk between the teeth. I pretended I needed to go to the bathroom, but I was really scrubbing her grubby comb.*

Kate's mother is all grown up now. Maybe she's figured out that scrubbing combs is not all that important. Other things matter more. She should tell Kate what these things are.

Why do we have to figure everything out for ourselves?

•

Fractals

•

•

WHENEVER SARAH GOES TO parties she comes home with brain ache. She worries about this. Has all her grey matter been used up? Is it beginning to disintegrate?

People talk about fractals as though the word is in her dictionary & the concept in her mind. They talk fractals faster than Sarah's mind can listen. Maybe her synapses are rusty; Sarah thinks she can hear them creak.

Sometimes people happen to bring fractal pictures with them. Sarah stares at the photographs & tries to understand how a complicated equation can be caught mid-calculation. She finds the colours garish, unbelievable, & thinks it's so unfair: people only bother with fractals that have dramatic coloration. Then reminds herself: of course not. The colours are from a range which has been arbitrarily selected. Sarah refuses to be seduced by beautiful blues & reds & purples. She demands black & white pictures, claims colour distracts from a fractal's perfect harmonious form. But the black & white photos are striking too.

Everyone seems to know about fractals. How did they find out? she wonders. Where was she when this happened? Probably yawning, listening to Ronnie pontificate. He talked academic in catch-phrases. He always referred to post-modernism as po-mo.

The year she discovered palimpsest, it suddenly seemed

profoundly true. She could feel how layers of meaning build on each other, like memory, deeper & deeper, richer. Sarah knew she could remove them like an onion, but didn't want to spoil the magic. The layers had always been building, of course, but now she noticed & rejoiced. For a while she thought palimpsest might change her life.

Deconstruction, post-modernism, post-post-modernism. These concepts seem quaint now, so commonplace that no one mentions them any more, luckily for Sarah who never understood them. But it doesn't matter: teachers think up new ones.

It is Saturday. Sarah soaks in the bathtub & reads the coloured comics, even though she only cares about the boy with a stuffed tiger that comes to life when grown-ups aren't around. She saves it to the last, like icing on chocolate cake. She reads the comics to keep from wondering which concept will be discussed tonight at Judy's party.

She worries anyway. Will she have to pretend she understands? Otherwise will people laugh? Sometimes when she admits she doesn't get it, it turns out that others don't either but have been waiting for someone else to say so first. Why am I always that person? Sarah wonders. She thumps her head against the wall like Charlie Brown. She'd say *Aaargh* like him too, if she knew how to pronounce it.

Finally Sarah can't put it off any longer. She has to get dressed for the party. It's the worst kind: there won't be any people she knows, except Judy. What kind of friends would Judy have? she wonders. Compulsive chartered accountants from the office where she works?

Sarah puts on eye shadow, then takes it off. It doesn't make her look intellectual. She wears her purple skirt & emerald sweatshirt & black stretch pants & fuchsia socks. Finally. All her other clothes have been tried on & rejected & tossed in a heap beside the bed. A tarnished silver box hangs from a leather thong around her neck. Sarah opens the container & stares at empty space. Someday she will place something inside it if she can ever think of what.

Her sister gave her the pendant last week to celebrate Sarah's break-up with Ronnie. Sarah tried it on. *It's beautiful. It looks ancient.*

It's supposed to look like an antique, Margie told her. *It's an imitation. Open it up.*

The pendant was actually a tiny box. Sarah studied the shape of the empty space inside. *What's it for?*

Poison, Margie told her, & they laughed, then got tipsy on the champagne Margie had brought to celebrate.

This is the first time Sarah has worn the pendant. She doesn't own any poison, except for cockroach chalk.

Sarah has to move everything in the junk drawer: motel soaps, incense sticks, ribbons left over from Christmas. Face-down, in a bristle of thumbtacks & picture hooks, is a snapshot of Ronnie. Sarah chops it into tiny pieces & fits them inside the necklace. There! she thinks. Perfect!

Judy's apartment is full of strangers who are loud & alcoholic, not like Sarah who drinks champagne on festive occasions, whenever she breaks up with a creep like Ronnie. People around her are smoking pot; Sarah doesn't toke at all.

Sarah notices the conversation is out-of-date; these people still argue post-modernism, which the loudest one calls po-mo. Sarah studies him. He's short & fat instead of tall & gawky. Otherwise he could be Ronnie. Sarah interrupts him & mentions fractals. The guests stare at her in amazement & ask, *How do you spell that word again? What in the world would they look like?* Sarah tells of beautiful patterns in blues & greens & purples. She apologizes for not bringing pictures.

Her hair is long these days, & shaggy because she always forgets to brush it. When Sarah pushes it out of her eyes her hand brushes against her head & she notices a lack of brain ache.

•

Babies Are Beautiful or Else They Aren't

•

•

CHARLOTTE DECIDED YEARS AGO never to have a baby. *The world doesn't need more people,* she'd said. *There are too many now,* Her sister said she was crazy. *What if our parents had felt that way? Where would we be?*

Maybe that's when Charlotte began to change her mind. Now she wants children but Martin still doesn't, insisting, *We decided about this before we got married. You can't change your mind.* He sounds so reasonable that Charlotte gets stubborn & wants kids even more.

Martin doesn't touch her very often, not since reading in a magazine that birth control pills are only 95% safe. The container is on the kitchen counter, the same as always. Each day Charlotte drops a pill in the kitchen sink as she washes the dishes.

Babies in strollers glide toward her on the street. Sometimes soothers are stuck inside their mouths like stoppers in a sink. Sometimes they holler for food or milk or because their diapers are cold & wet. Sometimes the sun is blinding their eyes. Charlotte thinks babies have a lot to holler about.

Also the lack of love. On a talk show Charlotte heard a psychologist mention there's not enough love to go around; people need a lot more than they'll ever get. Charlotte starts crying; she knows it's true.

She watches old people on the street. Exhausted old women with flattened breasts, their faces creasing into mirror images of their grandmothers & maiden aunts. *Did you get enough love to last a lifetime?* she wants to ask them, or, *How did you adjust to not getting enough?* She needs to know.

Charlotte knows she has enough love to give a baby.

Charlotte's friend works in a hospital nursery & cuddles ugly babies every chance she gets. She doesn't bother with the others. *The homely ones might not get enough cuddling later,* she says. *I worry about what their lives will be like.*

All babies are beautiful, Charlotte tells her, a trifle smugly, but her friend offers to bring pictures.

Charlotte watches her sister have a baby. *You might as well,* her sister tells her. *This may be as close to a delivery room as you'll ever get.* Charlotte expected birth to be beautiful, with subdued lighting, soft music to welcome the tiny new arrival to the world. Now she wonders how she could ever have been so naive. Her sister is screaming, screaming, screaming, determined not to, but screaming anyway. Her husband keeps reminding her to breathe, over & over like a broken record. Charlotte wants to tell him to shut up. The child is stuck cross-ways inside the womb. *Stubborn little bugger,* says the doctor in an admiring voice. He orders it, *Give up, kid. You've got to come out sooner or later. You'd might as well get it over with,* & finally the baby does.

Will the child remember? Charlotte wonders. Surely that memory must be imprinted on its brain, impossible to forget. Certainly its parents will never forget. Charlotte won't either.

Now Charlotte wonders about her own birth. Surely that memory must linger, even though she has somehow blocked it out. Maybe all her fears date back to that terrible time.

A neighbour claims to remember before he was born. *It was so peaceful floating in the womb,* he says. But Charlotte has seen birth happen. *What about the contractions?* she wants to ask. *The uterine muscles squashing your head?* She doesn't ask though, not wanting to disturb his dreamy faraway look. She's such a coward.

But she does finally confront Martin about their sexless nights. *Are you sleeping with someone else?* she yells. As soon as she asks she knows it's true. Of course. He must be. Martin denies it & Charlotte pretends to believe him, but it's over & they both know it. Love & trust & passion gone. She feels the loss like an amputation. When he moves out it's an anticlimax.

Charlotte quits her job at the stock exchange & works in a day care centre instead. She cuddles little children whether they are beautiful or not. The homely ones get extra hugs.

•

Brenda & Rev. Meadows

•

•

BRENDA & REV. MEADOWS disobeyed Momma & God. Now Brenda walks along the beach. She is under surveillance. Seagulls circle around her, like TV cameras in convenience stores, keeping her in focus. Brenda stares back at those seagulls to show she's not afraid.

A stranger walks toward her on the beach. Brenda grabs his arm as he walks past. *They breed us, you know,* she tells him. *For experiments, the same way we breed white mice. They can remove one of us whenever they want to. We're like cells inside a test tube or chickens in a coop.*

Right, he says.

They fitted the houses & streets together, the same way little kids fit building blocks & train tracks.

He shrugs her hand off & walks on. *You remind me of him,* she hollers, but the man walks faster.

She has the same sex dream over & over, & keeps mumbling it under her breath: the Reverend Meadows dream:

He seemed so proper & religious & old & ugly, preaching goodness from the pulpit, so after choir practice it would be okay to climb inside his car & not be nervous. But later we tiptoed up to my bed, Momma such a sound sleeper, never hearing anything once her head touches that goose-down pillow.

He kissed the soles of my feet & I quivered whenever he touched me. I was like a ukulele & he played me all night & oh I sang, oh I made wild frantic gypsy music.

Our bodies dancing, an ancient song playing deep inside us. We sang that song together, the notes falling perfectly into place, like Amazing Grace.

We swam around each other like mating dolphins. We sang our dolphin words & understood them. Our bodies curled together after, like we were sleeping inside the rocking cradle of the sea.

I was so beautiful & he was, as though those old-time alchemists had touched us & we'd turned gold. I knew everywhere to touch him & knew how to make him happy. He tried to braid my private hair. He kissed my secret place & he touched it with his tongue.

That's the way my momma found us, then started to shriek. Only fifteen years old! Screaming it over & over. Only fifteen years old!

Momma says he's gone far away, but that train whistle is like a phone call I'm making to him somewhere. Calling, Come on back. Come on back to me again. Oh please come back.

That lonesome train sound at night. Inside the sleeping-car berths people make love all the way from one station to the next. Their shadows against the curtains moving up & down, up & down, like those old handcars in silent movies. That freedom. The rumble of the train as it tunnels through the dark with its hot exploring tongue.

Don't try to tell me it was a sin.

Momma says he never loved me but I don't care. For a little while I was beautiful & I know he felt beautiful too.

Momma watches me all the time now. She locks me into my room at night. She aims her binoculars at me as I walk along the beach.

God uses seagulls.

•

Bright Butterflies Are Poisonous

•

•

SHIRLEY IS TALKING ABOUT BUTTERFLIES. *The bright ones are poisonous*, she says, *& their caterpillars are too. That's why birds don't eat them. Burt gave me a survival guide for my birthday & it tells which insects are safe to eat.*

As if we care.

It's a virus, says Melissa. *An epidemic*. She's talking about couples breaking up. Her friends fall out of love these days. They glance up & notice they're not with the right person, then start asking the same questions over & over: *What happened? How come we got together in the first place? Have we anything in common?* Melissa says the virus is infectious.

My friends fall out of love too. They tell me all about it because they think it makes me happy. *See?* they're really saying, *It's not just you & Wendell. We're going through the same thing.*

How about you? Melissa asks Shirley. *Are you & Burt okay?*

They'd better be. They're a perfect match. They're the only couple I know with a Hudson Bay blanket for a bedspread. They wear matching fishing vests with lots of pockets & buy each other thermal underwear for Christmas. *You can't survive on rabbits. They don't have the vitamins you need.* This is the sort of thing they mention in Burger Heaven over cheeseburgers &

fries. Or, *If a filling falls out of your tooth just plug the cavity with pine-gum.* Do they think we care about this stuff? *The grubs under rocks are a source of protein.* Shirley & Burt had better stay together; they haven't a hope of finding anyone else the same.

Shirley says, *Yeah, we're okay,* but her voice sounds doubtful. Maybe they're human after all.

We talk about Melissa's virus idea & laugh. I tell Melissa she's wrong. It's love that's the virus. Breaking up cures it like penicillin.

Shirley says, *No. Breaking up must be more like an antidote. It's so specific,* & then she explains about antivenin for rattlesnake bites.

Snake-talk makes us think of Eve & all that guilt.

Gay couples are breaking up too, Melissa says, & tells about a guy she knows at work.

I confide about my sister. She walked out on my brother-in-law last month but left her little boy behind. Mom & Dad had a fit. *You can't abandon our grandchild,* they told her, & offered to take him themselves, maybe even adopt him.

Don't be crazy, my sister told them. *He's already got two parents, but he needs some grandparents too. That's what you two are supposed to be.* She has strong ideas about grandparents. They're supposed to love the kid, & make sure he knows it, no matter what.

Mom was frantic & kept wailing, *Why does everything happen to me? It isn't fair. I can't take it.* I waited for Dad to joke her out of it but instead he said, *I can't take it either.* I looked at them & suddenly noticed they've turned old.

Everyone divorces these days, I tell Shirley & Melissa. *Everyone divorces at least once.*

The couple downstairs are seeing a counsellor. Luci told me, *We're only going so we won't blame ourselves later, to prove we really tried. We want the counsellor to say it's okay to give up.*

I know, I said, & of course I do.

Anyway, she said, *we never should have got married in the first place. We've nothing in common. You must have noticed. Why didn't you warn me?*

I tried to defend myself. *You wouldn't have listened. You were crazy in love. Reg this, Reg that. If I'd said anything you'd have dropped me as a friend.*

What about my mother then? She must have known.

C'mon, Luci, I said, *be reasonable. Parents don't choose who their kids marry. We get to make our own mistakes.*

Yeah. But I wasted years of my life. Maybe I'd have been happy with someone else.

Like who? I asked, but she didn't know. I told her, *No, you'd have found another guy just like him. It wouldn't have changed a thing.*

But now my daughter is getting married. She expects me to be happy about it, as if I'm ever happy about weddings.

When my friends break up I can reassure them things will get better. *It's bad but you get over it & life gets better. It's easier than being in a bad marriage & pretending everything's fine.* But when people get married what can I say? *It gets worse. You're happy now but you'll get over it.* I can't tell them that.

I want to say things to my daughter. *Okay. I can get used to the guy you've chosen. But do yourself a favour. Don't have any kids.* But then she'd have a few just to spite me. I know; that's why I had her.

I guess my ex will come to Toronto for the wedding, maybe even give her away, that quaint patriarchal custom. My mother & father will be crying. Another marriage to cross their fingers about.

My sister's kid will be dressed up in his first suit. People will gush that he's adorable & well-behaved. They'll notice he looks like his dad, & wonder whether it's okay to say it. That's rough for Tracy. I think about her watching her child grow up, looking more & more like the guy she fell out of love with, like a bad memory or recurring dream, like a sore tooth your tongue returns & returns to.

That reminds me of pine gum for toothache on camping trips. Shirley & Burt. Their life seems simple, maybe because they don't have kids.

Shirley & Burt hike through the woods. At first the forest seems silent, but soon they notice rustling & chirping sounds. When they sit down for lunch small animals come close. Butterflies land on their shoulders. Or maybe I've got them mixed up with Adam & Eve.

•

These Days They Live Inside a House with Slanted Floors

•

•

THIS HOUSE HAS A PORCH with criss-cross slats along the bottom. Sometimes Norrie squeezes behind the steps & crawls inside. Sunlight makes diamond patterns on the ground & on her legs.

She is invisible & watches everything that happens. Sometimes a boy throws a newspaper that bangs the floor above her head. Sometimes a woman with curlers & a kerchief pushes a baby carriage up & down the next-door driveway. The baby screams; the mother screams back.

Norrie pokes an old popsicle stick down a june-bug hole, then yanks out a big beetle that holds on tight with its sharp pincers. She drops the stick in a pickle jar & watches for a while before letting the june-bug go. Then she pokes her stick down another hole, & so on.

Norrie hears Momma's splintery voice call & call her name. Then the slam of the screen door as Momma goes back inside, muttering, *Dammit, dammit, dammit, that lazy kid.* Momma hasn't discovered the hiding place beneath the porch but Norrie knows it is only a matter of time.

The other good thing about this house is the slanty floor. Norrie rolls marbles from the front hall into the kitchen. Sometimes Momma trips over them, maybe falls down with a clunk, sometimes breaks dishes, sometimes just lies there crying, *Mygod, mygod, mygod, what a stupid kid.*

This time Momma falls & drops a bottle. Norrie watches brown liquid drizzle along the slanty floor & disappear under the baseboard. Momma snatches the bottle & looks inside; almost nothing left. *Dammit,* Momma hollers. *That's my medicine! I gotta have it.*

Momma grabs hold of the kitchen table & drags herself up from the floor. Her hand swats Norrie's head & then the bumblebee sound is back again. Momma's words inside the buzz, *Skip supper then. Bzzz. That'll fix you. Bzzz. Get up to your room. I'll tell your daddy when he gets home from work. Bzzz. Just you wait!*

Norrie waits for Daddy. She hears Momma bang pots & pans. Cupboard doors slam. She smells food cooking, then smells it burn. Chicken maybe. Fried chicken is Norrie's favourite.

A car stops in the driveway. Screen door skreeks open. Voices yelp inside the kitchen. Then Daddy stomps up the stairs. At school the big kids play *Three Billy Goats Gruff.* They make fierce faces & stamp their feet. Daddy's feet sound just like that.

Daddy rolls his sleeves up. He takes his time. Norrie looks at the dark hairs on his arms. She has never seen him comb them.

Daddy hollers, *Okay kiddo. This time you're really going to get it! Your momma & I are both fed up! What'll it be? The razor strap or my belt?* His words bang like firecrackers against Norrie's ears.

Whichever Norrie says, he grabs the other. *Too bad then,* he yells. *You like the razor strap better? Okay then, I'll use my belt! Pull your pants down!*

Norrie grabs her underpants & holds on tight. Daddy grabs her by the arm. Norrie dances around him, trying to pull away. *No Daddy! Please! No! No! No!*

Daddy throws her down on the bed & yanks her pants off. Norrie is screaming.

I'll fix you, young lady, he hollers. *I'll beat Satan right out of your bones. Make him slink out your bedroom door with his tail & pitchfork dragging. Let him find some other little girl to wind around his finger.*

No, Daddy! No!

Then Daddy mutters, *Hurry up now. Yell louder.*

He swats the belt against his bare arm & Norrie screams as loud as she can. She tries to grab the belt away, but Daddy swats his arm again. Norrie screams, *No, Daddy! Oh please! Please stop it! I'll be good!*

Daddy flops down on her bed & holds his arm out. Norrie pulls down his white sleeve, covers up the black hairs & broken skin. She cries in gulps like hiccups, & can't see to fit the button inside the buttonhole. She rubs her arm against her face, wipes the tears & snot away.

Daddy just lies there.

I'm sorry, I'm sorry, Norrie keeps saying. *I'm sorry Daddy. I'll be good.*

All right then, says Daddy. *Touch me. You know the place.*

Bright red specks of blood make a connect-the-dots pattern on Daddy's shirt-sleeve.

•

Candles Burn in Churches & Restaurants & in Hospitals in the Crimea

•

•

PERHAPS HE IS DEAD. He is silent. It's been three days now & she wonders what to do.

Friday night he played the piano, the last sound she can remember. She sat in her armchair by the wall with her knitting, but the sad melody was so upsetting that she dropped stitches & gave up. She looks at the abandoned knitting in her basket. Beige angora, like the dust balls beneath her bed.

Three days. On Saturday afternoon she went for groceries at the market but wasn't gone more than an hour. She curses the way her body keeps needing groceries, week after week after week. Perhaps something happened while she was gone. Perhaps he coughed, called out, fell to the floor clutching his chest. She has thrown the groceries into the garbage. If she tried to eat them she would choke.

She should notify someone, her landlord maybe, or the police.

If she'd been home she would have heard him, would have broken in somehow & come to his rescue. She remembers a photograph of Florence Nightingale, her face sad from watching men in pain. Her long white dress. Her candle.

He looks up & sees her, & finds her as beautiful as old photographs of a nurse in the Crimea. *Tell me your name,* he asks, & she does.

It is Monday. She has listened beside the wall all day. She phoned in sick so she could do this. It's all over. He has moved away or he is dead. She will have to find someone new to dream of.

Her head is throbbing. She'll treat herself to dinner out. A distraction. Anyway the groceries are in the garbage; the cupboard's empty.

A man sits in the restaurant alone. She has seen him in the neighbourhood before, at the cleaners, perhaps, or in the grocery store or library. She remembers his light brown beard, how it is softening into grey. He wears a dark jacket, dark turtleneck. Perhaps he is an artist.

The waiter seats her at a nearby table so they face one another. She tries not to watch the man as he eats French onion soup, Caesar salad, a crisp white roll. He reads a newspaper as he eats, folding the pages in half lengthwise. She sees men do this each morning on the streetcar, conserving space.

Couples sit at all the other tables.

Beyond the clink of dishes & silver, classical music is playing. She has heard the piece before, but can't remember what it's called. The man sips at his glass of white wine.

She orders an omelette. *Salad? No, thank you*. The waiter leaves.

Perhaps she has seen him in rush hour on the streetcar.

The waiter seems to know him. They chat briefly about something. If she returns to this restaurant there's a good chance she'll see him again. Perhaps the next time she will order the same food as he does. He will be startled & pay attention.

She thinks the music must be a concerto. It changes a little & then continues. She wonders about the difference between a sonata & concerto. She thinks a concerto is much longer. The next time she's at the library she must remember to look this up.

It is summer. His face & hands are tanned. Probably his arms are too. She imagines the dividing line on his upper arm: below it, his summer tan; above, the natural colour of his skin. She would like to run her tongue along that line.

The man sits sideways in his chair & reads the paper. Perhaps he's shy & does this to avoid eye contact.

Or no. If she sees him here again she will not order the same meal as he does. It would draw his attention. He might strike up a conversation that could go anywhere.

The waiter seats another man at a nearby table. This must be the section where they seat all the single misfits, she thinks. The new man is younger, closer to her own age. She feels how he watches her as he pretends to read his magazine. She turns sideways to avoid him, & to concentrate on the bearded man who ignores her, who does not bore her, who orders coffee & raspberry sherbet.

His tanned hands, strong but gentle, brown against the pale skin of her body. He will compare her to some white flower, a daisy or snowdrop or gardenia.

They lie on a hillside. He removes her garments one by one, like petals from a daisy. *She loves me, she loves me not, she loves me...*

When his dessert arrives it is the colour of deep red claret. He eats it nonchalantly, as though he does this every day.

On each table a candle flickers in a small glass, like a shot glass, like a medicine glass without the calibrated markings. Why must she think this? She tries not to.

She remembers a ward. A nurse brings pills in a small glass. *Put the pills in your mouth, dear. That's right.* The nurse pours water into the glass & then says, *Swallow. Good. Now open your mouth. Lift up your tongue & let me see. If you don't swallow your pills we'll have to put the needle back in your arm. We'd have to do it for your own good.*

If she could choose what to remember she would forget this. She would also forget fathers & brothers & boyfriends.

The music has a pattern, like everything. Quickly, & then slowly. Sprightly. There are musical terms for this. Italian, maybe. Words she can't remember. After school an old man smells like cigar butts. He sits beside her on a piano bench & hits her small fingers with a ruler, because of those terms she can't remember. He bangs the ruler against the edge of the piano to keep time. It is years since she has seen him. Twenty years, maybe more. Is he alive? She hopes not. What was his name? It is years since she has thought of him at all.

It is not years since she has thought of him, but if she makes herself think so, then perhaps it will be. She pretends this.

The waiter pours the man a second cup of coffee, & then pours her one, as though they are together. The man rereads sections of his newspaper. He hates to leave. It is obvious to her. A less sensitive person would not notice.

She imagines the flat he must return to. It is neat enough, but lacks the little touches a woman makes. Sometimes he hates to return there. This is one of those times. She understands. It is sometimes the same for her.

Finally he can't put it off any longer. He folds his paper, gets up to leave.

On the way home perhaps she will burn a candle in the cathedral. There's no reason for her to stay now. She gathers her purse & glasses together, her knitted gloves, unread paperback. She's afraid that in a moment she will cry. Lately she sometimes does this for no reason.

Her eyes blur. She begins to open the washroom door. The waiter calls to her. *It's all right,* she tells him, *I left the money on the table.* As she opens the door she feels the waiter's hand on her shoulder. *No,* he says.

The man with the beard stands at a urinal. He sees her & looks surprised. A golden stream of urine wavers, stops, & then resumes.

•

Jancey & the Moon

•

•

JANCEY IGNORES THE OTHER people in the waiting room. She smooths the hem of her pink dress so it covers her knees. Pastel dresses are her trademark. Every day she wears them to the office where she is secretary to chartered accountants. When it's nearly time for her period she switches to dark clothes. Everyone knows when she expects it.

The men in the office know when it comes. Jancey winces, & at first pretends it's nothing, then says she's sorry, she'll have to hurry home & lie down. *All my life I've had bad cramps with my period*, she confides. She hangs her head down as she says this, & reminds him, whichever man it is, of his wife or his sister or girlfriend. Of course they give her as much time off as she needs. Poor little thing, she imagines them thinking.

They must find it so mysterious. Jancey thinks about them wondering, but never understanding, what goes on inside her female body & female mind, the way she's in tune with nature & surges with changes of the moon, just like the sea.

Jancey thinks of her uterus as a perfect little nursery she gets ready once a month & then dismantles. As though her body is always hopeful & grows another egg each month in case sperm should happen by. Jancey hasn't slept with a man since her last lover returned to his wife. She hasn't had sperm inside her body for five years, but of course her ovaries can't know this. They don't know there's no point making eggs.

Jancey buys tampons at the drug store by the office or anywhere that's handy. *Wait a sec,* she says to friends after supper or a movie, *I'd better buy a box of tampons before I forget.* She buys mini-pads as well, for the days before she gets her period, just in case.

Jancey keeps them handy in her desk. Women from other offices borrow tampons or mini-pads whenever they run out. Word gets around. Jancey is everybody's friend. They tell her to borrow back whenever she needs to, but Jancey never runs out; she's careful not to. She keeps a tampon in her purse, even when she's wearing pastel dresses & it's too early for her period. Her friends think this is silly, but Jancey finds it reassuring to know she has one handy & often reaches in her purse to be sure it's really there.

Sometimes she dumps everything out of her purse to find a missing subway token, & a tampon rolls onto a cafeteria counter along with everything else. Other women might be embarrassed, but never Jancey. She says, *This is part of what it is to be a woman,* & smiles at strangers who quickly look away.

Jancey feels sorry for men; their hormones are so ordinary. Every day is like another. There's no drama or fluctuation. *It's lucky your jobs are more exciting,* she consoles them. *It helps make up.*

Her age is anybody's guess & Jancey's secret. She imagines people pondering this question whenever she's not around & hopes she's fooled them into thinking she's five or ten years younger. Her figure's trim. She plays tennis every weekend & swims Tuesdays & Thursdays after work. Canada's Food Rules are taped to her refrigerator door. She sleeps eight hours each night. Her hair is touched up before it needs it. She wears whatever outfit is in fashion. Are there other things she ought to do? she wonders. She searches women's magazines in case there's something she's forgotten.

It's Jancey's turn. *Back again?* the doctor asks. *I saw you just last month.*

Jancey hates her doctor, although she knows it's unfair. She would hate anyone who happened to be her doctor & wrote down her answers to private questions.

What's the problem?

Jancey has no words to explain it. She's afraid to look at her body, afraid she'll see it dissolve into the body of an old lady like her mother or her aunt. Each time she glances into a mirror another change begins to happen.

Any trouble with bowel or bladder function? Nausea? Digestive problems?

Are her shoulders getting hunched? But hasn't she always had round shoulders?

Headaches? Dizzy spells?

She studies blemishes on the back of her hands. They look like freckles, but probably aren't. Skin is thin there. Brown spots lurk inside the skin & push up toward the surface. They seem to darken as she watches.

The doctor leans back & stares. Jancey wonders who he sees.

Forty's a little early for the menopause, but you're having an easy transition. No hot flushes. No other problems. The words sound familiar; Jancey hears them each time she comes.

She remembers being a child on Hallowe'en, the strange sensation of turning into someone else. This is happening again. How can she prevent it & return to the person she was before? She already swims, rides a bicycle, plays tennis. There must be some essential information the doctor has forgotten to pass on.

He keeps talking. *Probably you're pretty safe, but keep up birth control precautions anyway. You don't want to risk getting pregnant. With no periods to miss, you wouldn't even know.*

Jancey tries to remember what the precautions used to be. A condom. Spermicidal jelly. It's been so long since these items were important. White wine. Classical music.

Would sex be different now? she wonders. Are other changes taking place inside her that only a lover would be aware of? Changes Jancey's never thought of & can't predict?

On her way home she stops off at a drug store & buys a box of tampons. She stacks it in the bathroom cupboard with the others.

•

Agnes Not Thinking of George

•

•

People named Agnes always go mad. Agnes reads this in a book of superstitions. The words jolt like electric shock. They stretch across the page like an omen, a message she can't miss. She tells no one about them.

Where did the book come from? she wonders. Did someone place it on the bookshelf so she would find it?

There's a new member in group today. His name is George. They sit in a circle, & tell him their names. When it is her turn, she says, *Agnes, Lamb of God.* They tell what happened since last week. She says, *Nothing.*

Now people say, *Help yourself to coffee, George. George* this, *George* that.

Agnes already knows the name George & doesn't want to hear it again. She'd rather hear a name she can delight in, with several syllables to vibrate against her vocal cords, a name vocal cords were made for. She holds her hand against her throat & says names slowly. *Gregory. Benjamin. Alexander.* The words rumble comfortably against her hand. She feels guilty & forces herself to say *George.* One terrible jolt & it is over.

The others watch & listen. They should mind their own business.

Agnes is grown up now & can say whatever she wants, or she can say nothing. She can sit & think beautiful thoughts. She can contemplate a light switch until she feels she understands it.

Light switches are so simple & unassuming & useful. People couldn't get along without them. Agnes often needs to replace cracked switch plates. She lingers in the hardware store touching sockets & wiring, amazed that people are brave enough to buy these things & know what to do with them once they get home.

The switch plates crack because she screws them on too tight. Better too tight than too loose, she always thinks. One extra twist of the screwdriver, then another. Because she imagines the screw gradually working loose, the plate falling off unnoticed, someone reaching out in the dark, fingers slipping into the switch box, touching an open wire. She never wants to have children in case this happens.

In the dark she sometimes touches George.

Beside the doorway of the meeting room is a switch plate of smooth beige plastic. A matching beige toggle switch is positioned exactly inside it. Two silver screws hold the plate in place. There are beautiful thoughts she could be thinking about this. She wants to contemplate the universe carefully, bit by bit, beginning with this light switch. When she reaches a higher level of understanding then life will become beautiful & make sense.

Agnes stares at the light switch & tries to think of George. He is real. Gregory & Benjamin & Alexander are only beautiful words.

George, she says aloud, because she ought to, first making sure her hand is not against her throat. She almost chokes. Georgie Porgie gets in the way, & all those English kings. Why do parents name their babies George?

Let's name it after rich old Uncle George. He's never had a child named after him before. He'll be tickled pink. The parents are joking at first, then gradually get used to the idea.

Or they decide after the child is born. They stare at a helpless newborn, & suddenly think, *George. Of course! George! What do you think, darling? Doesn't the baby look like a perfect George? Hang it all, let's do it. Our friends will get such a laugh. Imagine their faces when they get the birth notice in the mail. They'll chortle, choke, spill cups of coffee, have to be swatted on their backs. They'll scream, George! Imagine! Parenthood will never change those two. They're still madcap as ever. Can you imagine anyone else calling a baby George?*

What would a perfect George-baby look like? Fat, like Georgie Porgie.

Georges say, *I only do this for your own good.* They do this to get even for their awful childhood. Bullies beat up pudgy boys named George. By the time the Georges are in their teens they're skinny & can fight back, but it's too late.

Sometimes Georges apologize.

All those English kings, numbered so people could keep track. Their subjects were the only ones who called them George. Those kings had other names at home. Friendly affectionate names. Like Bertie.

Agnes pictures the beautiful wife of George the Sixth. Every morning she puts on her pearl necklace & her smile. Two little daughters follow her around, dressed in matching skirts of Harris tweed & matching sweaters of Shetland wool. They play quietly like princesses should. When the king gets home from work, his beautiful wife tells him to sit down & rest. *Poor Bertie. You look all tuckered out from running your kingdom. Relax. I'll make a nice cup of English tea. Put your feet up & have a rest. Stop being George until tomorrow.*

Or was Bertie the other one, the older brother with the tough American wife? *Bertie. Don't just sit there. Make me tea & crumpets. Also hot buttered scones. Don't forget the Devonshire cream.*

Anyway, never George. Royals never say the George-word aloud. They print it on birth certificates, along with a dozen other names. Kings sign George on royal documents. Their subjects adore them & name their babies George. Whenever a king receives a letter addressed to George he knows he can ignore it. It's only fan-mail. Another loyal subject has named a baby after him. The royal secretary sends off a form letter in reply.

Agnes sucks on a lozenge because her throat is sore from saying, *George, George, George!*

She thinks there used to be a wrestler named Gorgeous George. Alliteration must be the reason why. Wrestlers beat people up. Sometimes Agnes wears dark glasses or stays inside.

Agnes still daydreams of a boy she watched in high school twenty years ago. She never knew his name. A stranger across a crowded room, like in the *South Pacific* song. He was reading a serious book, then looked up at her & smiled. He walked toward her. His name was Gregory or Benjamin or Alexander.

Georges chop down cherry trees & admit it. They slay dragons to save fair maidens. Agnes used to be a fair maiden herself.

Someone says, *Agnes, you're awfully quiet. Do you want to talk about your husband?*

She says she can't remember his name.

•

Crib Death

•

•

NICK'S MOTHER REMEMBERS SOMETHING NEW. *You died in August*, she tells him. Nick shudders. Each time she tells this story she adds more details.

The first time they're driving along some highway. His mother's behind the wheel, so he must be under sixteen; once he got his licence she stopped driving. Sunshine in the side window is making him sleepy. Country music from the car radio lazily throbs against his mind. Then the news: Viet Nam war, a mail strike, a crib death. He thinks of old men playing cribbage & asks her, *Hey, Mom. What's a crib death?* A long silence. Then her voice sounds small & far away, *You died when you were a baby.*

He wonders what on earth she's talking about. Can she possibly be talking to him? About him? The car hurtles faster along a grey highway that goes nowhere. Nick thinks his mother must be going crazy, & he wonders what it feels like. Does it hurt? Is it okay for her to drive a car while this happens? The sun is shining. Fields of cows & horses keep sliding behind them.

You're joking, right?

So she tells him a story & he tries to picture it like a TV show: a baby lying on its back inside a playpen, an older brother at the kitchen table finishing his dinner, the mother starting to wash dishes.

You'd been playing with a rattle, she says. *You'd already had dinner. Probably mashed banana. You always liked it best.* She pauses as though he's supposed to make some comment. Then, *You were only six months old,* she says.

Nick imagines lying helpless on his back, high wooden slats fenced all around him, the kitchen ceiling far above.

You were such a sweet baby. Remind me to get out the photo album when we get home.

Never mind. Just tell me what happened.

I glanced over & noticed you'd dropped off to sleep, but something seemed wrong, I'm not sure what. I grabbed you & held you upside down & pounded your back till you started to breathe.

That's it? You mean I stopped breathing for no reason, & then just started to breathe again? Just like that? It's hard to breathe right now, his chest & belly tight.

I was scared to let you out of my sight after that.

Nick looks at green fields outside the car window, he looks at sky. Clouds bulge like puffy snowmen inside that bright blue sky.

It was years ago, she says. *You were a tiny baby, but whenever I hear about a crib death it comes back. I still get goose-bumps. Let's change the subject.*

She shouldn't want to forget it, Nick thinks; it's too important. *What about Tim?* he asks.

Tim was eating his dinner.

I mean, did it ever happen to Tim?

No. It's pretty rare.

Landscape slips past, a donut shop, a gas station, a motel, as though nothing has changed, as though the world keeps spinning round & round, no matter what happens on its surface.

Years pass before she mentions it again. They're babysitting Tim & Cindy's child. *Don't ever ask me to babysit,* his mother had told them right from the start. *I've raised my own kids. Now it's your turn.*

At first Cindy could hardly believe it. *Grandmothers are supposed to love little babies,* she'd protested. But it didn't bother Tim. He & Nick had heard it again & again while they were growing up. Whenever a young woman moved back home with a baby, whenever her friends bragged about their grandchildren. *You'll be on your own,* their mother had always said. *Don't count on me.*

But this is an emergency: Cindy's father dies. They have to ask her & she can't refuse. She makes Nick stay home all evening with her.

It's Friday night, Ma. You must be kidding. But she isn't. He takes his coat off when she starts crying, because she's a woman who doesn't cry.

I was ready to leave for night school, cleaning up the kitchen before the babysitter came. What if I'd already left? If she'd been there would she have noticed something was wrong? I don't think so. I worry about that. I don't even know why I noticed myself.

She's huddled in the corner of the chesterfield, her eyes open, but focused on some place inside her mind. *Do you want some tea?* she suddenly asks, but doesn't move. Finally Nick makes it himself.

You looked limp. I picked you up quick & you just hung there, heavy, lifeless. I could tell you'd already left. I held you upside-down anyway. It wasn't easy. You were six months old, big & sturdy, but somehow I held you upside-down with one hand &

banged the other against your back. Over & over. Like having a tug-of-war with angels. Finally they let go & you came back. I don't think the doctors believed me. They didn't say so but I could tell. But they weren't inside that kitchen, didn't hold you like a rag doll & know you'd gone.

She rubs her arms as though she's cold. She hasn't touched her tea. Nick makes another pot. When he puts the cup beside her she looks startled. *You weren't sick. Never even had a sniffle.*

Finally she falls asleep & Nick covers her with a blanket. He unrolls his sleeping bag on the floor beside his nephew's crib & listens for breathing sounds.

Next night the baby's still with them & she makes him stay home again. *At the hospital they said you had pneumonia. Early pneumonia. They found it on the X-ray. You were in an oxygen tent for days. I'd sit beside your bed, realizing how fragile all our lives were. I felt so helpless. I'd saved you this time, but what about the next?*

Tim & Cindy return, pick up their baby, & never ask her to babysit again.

When Nick's wife gets pregnant, his mother says right from the beginning, *Don't count on me to babysit. I can't do it.*

Jilly complains to Nick, *It'll be stupid to put the baby into daycare when your mother lives right around the corner. Once the baby comes she'll change her mind.*

Jilly's labour seems to take forever. Nick holds her hand & rubs her back, learns how to pray. Now he & his mother look through the nursery window. The baby is tiny & defenceless. Nick feels frightened but knows it's okay; all new fathers feel the same way. *Hey Mom, isn't he something! Who do you think he looks like? Jilly or me?*

It was a Monday, she says. *Be careful Mondays.*

•

Her Children Keep On Having Conversations Anyway

•

•

SOMEONE DREAMS OF SOMEONE who dreams of someone else, & so on. A woman dreams that she is dead. Or she IS dead, & keeps on dreaming. She just lies there. Life goes on around her. Conversations. Her children's voices:

Good thing Momma didn't see this newscast, says Ruth. *Police not swearing allegiance to Queen Elizabeth any more. She'd have been mad.*

Then Ed's voice. *Yeah. Her whole generation. When I was a kid she took me to see someone in the royal family. We waited for hours on the sidewalk. Finally an open car came by. Some woman wearing white gloves waved to the crowd. Maybe a princess or the queen, I can't remember.*

Didn't the princess ride in a coach? Marlene asks. *Like in a fairy tale?*

Ed sighs. *Not a coach with horses. No. Just a car without a roof.* He waits, but Marlene doesn't ask anything else. She is pulling grey hairs from her head. With every yank she chants, *He loves me,* or else, *He loves me not.*

Ed continues, *All those monarchists are dying off. Why should we swear allegiance to some phony foreign queen? It's ridiculous. Those Windsors are no better than anyone else.*

The woman lies there dreaming she's dead. As if I care, she thinks. As if it matters whether police swear allegiance to anyone. Whether judges swear, or anyone else. Making promises doesn't mean you'll keep them. She is thinking about marriage.

History matters though, says Ruth, who took it all through high school. *I still remember all those English kings & queens.* She starts to recite them.

Marlene is is humming God Save the Queen. *I like that old song,* she says. *You get a chance to stand up & sing.*

Gone like the dodo, says Ruth. *Just as well. Gone with the Lord's Prayer & the strap & inkwells.*

Remember pen-wipers? Ed asks, but no one does. That's the trouble with being the oldest, he thinks as he starts to explain, *We had to bring a piece of flannel to wipe our pen nibs.*

What are pen nibs? asks Marlene.

Ruth can't remember pen wipers. She doesn't believe in them or anything else she hasn't read about in books. She thinks it isn't fair: important things from her own life are missing from her mind, but she still knows the date of the Battle of Hastings & the names of all the wives of Henry the Eight. Those memories are fading too though, but Ruth can still cover up her memory lapses. She smiles, says, *Pen wipers. I'd almost forgotten,* in a gentle dreamy voice.

The old woman lies on the worn sofa in her kitchen, her cat stretched out beside her. She is dreaming of cats; they don't need to swear allegiance, they rub against your legs & purr, they curl up on your lap whenever you sit down in the rocker. Allegiance. Cats could teach us a thing or two, the old woman thinks. She tries to say it aloud but is unable.

I can't believe she's gone, says Ed. *It doesn't feel like she's missing. Mamma was always quiet, but I could feel her in the room, feel what she was thinking. I still can feel it.*

She hasn't gone anywhere, says Ruth. *Look how the cat lies at the edge of the sofa, in the same spot as always, leaving room for Momma against the wall.*

The old woman listens & wonders which one's right. Is she dead or isn't she? Should she pinch herself? What would it prove?

Come here Tiger, Marlene calls. The cat doesn't move, so she grabs it & holds on tight. *Stupid cat. You're supposed to come when I call you. It's a rule.*

Rules change, Marlene, Ed warns her. *Everything changes.*

Even us?

They were such cute babies, the woman remembers. Especially Marlene; her big blue eyes & innocent expression. *Borderline,* the teachers called her. Except once, when the principal said, *She's slow. You've got to accept it,* & her daddy knocked him down. Pa couldn't get away with it these days, the woman thinks, but no one sided with the principal then. Neighbours stuck together. No little twit with a fancy education could call one of them dumb. He'd said slow, but dumb was what he meant.

Marlene has grey hair now & still looks innocent. She looks normal, the woman thinks, & maybe she really is. She cooks & cleans & launders, earns a decent living. These days women would rather run errands at an office & have Marlene wash their clothes & dishes while they're gone. Ed's right, the woman thinks. Everything does change.

Ed had to stay home & work the farm after his pa had a stroke. Who else could do it? & Marlene had to live at home too. Someone had to keep an eye on her. She was like a little kitten. She'd let any stranger pat her, would rub up against him & start purring. The minister said no to all that; maybe he was right, maybe he wasn't, but they believed him & kept her away from men.

That husband dead so long now, almost twenty years ago. That old man, almost as old as her father, a widower who needed her to raise his kids. She can hardly remember what he looked like. Is he up there waiting for her? Wearing a heavenly gown? The sleeves too short to cover his spindly arms? Does he sing celestial hymns in his twangy off-key voice? He can just keep right on waiting. She would shrivel up from boredom. She'll stay right here on this couch in her own kitchen as long as she can, a patchwork quilt underneath her, the log cabin pattern stitched by her mother; a crocheted afghan on top.

Look at her, says Ruth. *Lying there so peaceful.* Oh thank heavens, the woman thinks. I'm alive after all. Ruth can see me. I've just been dreaming. But it turns out Ruth is talking about the cat.

•

Flying

•

•

EDDIE SITS ON THE BALCONY RAILING, his feet dangling back & forth, casting shadows on the balcony below. A door bangs open & Mrs Anderson peers up.

Eddie! O my goodness, Eddie, you gave me a scare. I saw a shadow moving. You know, out of the corner of my eye. At first I thought it was a bird. Then I was scared it was a burglar. What are you doing up there anyway? Are you safe? I wouldn't sit on the railing for anything. You know me. Even the elevator gives me palpitations. I was telling my doctor the other day …

I'm fine.

Well, okay then, if you're sure. I'm watching the soaps. Jeremy's all alone with the girl he really likes. I think he might propose. Come down & watch it.

I'm busy. Thanks anyway.

Eddie will pass Mrs Anderson's balcony first. Maybe she will look up from her soaps, maybe she won't. She'll tell people about it later, how real life imitates TV. On the big screen outside her window dramas keep happening.

* * *

The blonde woman will be sunbathing in the nude. From the air

Eddie will finally be able to see her. He'll wave, give a wolf whistle to show his appreciation. Maybe he'll say, *Hubba, hubba,* so she'll realize he's really a nice old-fashioned guy. She'll grab a towel & cover her breasts & crotch. He could take along his camera & aim it as he passes. There's no film, but she won't know that. *Nice,* he'll tell her. *Real nice.* He'll say it slow.

* * *

Cindy will be home from school. She'll be sipping from a pop can through coloured straws, a bowl of buttered popcorn beside her, a teen romance novel open on her lap

The phone will ring, her girlfriend across the courtyard hollering, *Look outside quick. You know that crazy guy on the top floor? The guy who tells us to hurry & grow up so he can marry us both? He's standing on his balcony railing & his arms are flapping up & down. He looks like he's trying to fly.*

Cindy will dash out onto the balcony, the bowl of popcorn still in her hand. He'll grab a handful as he glides by. He'll mind his manners & holler, *Thanks.*

* * *

Old Mr Stovanovich will be dozing on his couch. Old Mrs Stovanovich will be knitting, probably a bonnet or booties for a new great-grandchild. A silver thread is twisted in the wool & it catches little pieces of the sun.

It's okay, Eddie will reassure her. *Pay attention to your knitting. Don't drop a stitch.*

Old Mr Stovanovich will be dreaming. In his dream he is sixteen years old again & hiking in the Alps with a young girl from school. Yellow flowers are all around them. It's a grand dream. He hears his wife screaming, but doesn't want to wake up.

* * *

Bernie's still out of work. Maybe he'll be reading the want ads or pounding pavement. Maybe flopped in bed with a pillow over his head or flicking lighted matches at the wall. Or visiting the woman down the hall, seeking comfort.

* * *

The man on the third floor plays a harmonica, the heartbreak blues. The music cries, *Waa waaa,* like a baby whose momma's gone away & left it. *Waa waaa waaaa.* That sad sound always makes Eddie want to cry. He hopes the harmonica man won't be there.

* * *

Mrs Kwan will be jiggling a stroller back & forth. She'll put a finger to her lips, & whisper, *Shhh. I just got the baby off to sleep.*

He's getting pretty big, Eddie will tell her.

Thirteen pounds, five & a half ounces, she'll say, smiling.

Wow! He'll be a football player when he grows up. Some day you'll watch him in the playoffs on TV.

Don't rush him, she'll say. *He'll take it one day at a time, just like the rest of us.*

She always says this. Like a reformed alcoholic. It's good advice. People should listen.

* * *

The fireman on the night shift will be asleep.

* * *

Eddie stands up on his railing & waves to Cindy's girlfriend across the courtyard.

He hears Mrs Anderson call, *Eddie! Guess what! Jeremy proposed! He finally did it! I think she might say yes!*

Eddie moves his arms slowly up & down. Blue sky fills in around them. Then he glides past all the balconies & forgets to look.

•

Plots

•

•

THERE AREN'T MANY STORIES.

My daughter showed me a book from her English class that claimed there are only about ten different plots. It listed them neatly on a page. All stories, it claimed, if you really pay attention, if you analyse them seriously, will fit into one or another. I wish I'd copied down that list.

Of course not, I told her, *We can make whatever choices we want. The possibilities are endless. There are as many stories as people.*

But I started to believe it, all the same. Later she read another article that said there were only half a dozen. As she told me I felt my life getting even more restricted. I guess I should have felt it coming. Finally she read a book that said those other analysts were wrong; there's only one story.

There aren't all that many really important things that happen. I keep on living & find that out. Here's my list:

1. Parents leave. The child is alone.
2. A lover leaves. The woman's alone.
3. Children leave. The mother's alone.

Only one story: a woman left all alone. This is from a female perspective of course.

The woman knows they'll leave her someday, so never dares get too attached to them. So, in a way, long before they leave, the woman's already alone, but she pretends she isn't. The pretending makes a difference.

Someone said life is a long series of goodbyes.

Today I scream at Wally, *Go ahead. See if I care. Walk out that door & don't come back*. He's so stupid sometimes. He walks out the door as though I mean it, as though he's been waiting for permission. We both know he's in the right. It's my fault. What else is new? It's always the woman's fault.

Wally, come back here, I want to holler. I want to, but I won't. I have some pride. A woman left all alone, she hasn't much, but she has her pride.

Anyway, I shouldn't have to call him back. Doesn't he know I need him? Doesn't he need me too?

He leaves because of my kids. No, he leaves because of me; because I was scared to tell my kids about him. I didn't want him to leave me, but didn't want them to abandon me either. I wanted it all. Of course. Who doesn't?

My earliest childhood memories are more like feelings. They hurt with a pain I got used to & can almost ignore. I can't share those memories because I have no language to express them. They happened before I had sufficient words. I can't prove those memories, but I believe them, which makes them true. I grew up & tried to understand all those old feelings, remembered in flickered glimpses, like a broken movie reel. Usually the dialogue is missing.

Eyewitnesses see an accident & each one gives a different version of what happened. A sunny day or spitting rain; red T-bird or grey Datsun or camouflage jeep; sped through a stop sign or stopped & looked in both directions. The child & the parent share memories like that.

My mother is wrecking my best stories. They're all I've kept from my childhood. I pull them out whenever I need to, & fiddle with them like Captain Queeg playing with ball bearings. But my mother tries to destroy them. I was born in 1948; that's all we can agree on. She doesn't realize my memories make me who I am; if I lose them I'll disappear. Or maybe she doesn't care. I suppose she needs her memories to be right or she'll disappear instead. She's older; she ought to go first.

It's the same with my kids. Things didn't happen the way they claim they did. If I slip & drown inside my bathtub my children will be free to remember whatever they want. Change the characters to change the plot & vice versa.

Sunday nights the kids come for supper & Wally leaves before they arrive. Then I check to make sure nothing masculine has been left lying around where anyone could notice. He always complains.

You don't understand, I tell him, & he always says, *Damn right!*

My kids were raised inside the church & they'd think we're living in sin. The church doesn't recognize divorce & neither do they. They think I'm still married to their father. If I slept with someone else I'd be committing adultery. They wouldn't stone me, like in the bible, but they'd abandon me, which is just as bad. My kids see it so simplistic. I understand. When I was young & had religion I thought the same way. Then I grew up.

Wally says I never did. It's easy for him. He didn't go to church three times each Sunday all through his childhood, plus extra meetings during the week.

He leaves. I check as always to make sure nothing of his is visible, & then notice: there's nothing left anywhere! Nothing at all!

He must have planned it ahead of time, & gradually moved out his possessions. He must have already found another place to live, & have another life in mind.

I can't believe it. I cry all afternoon instead of cooking the usual fancy Sunday dinner. The kids will abandon me too. It's only a matter of time. They've moved out already, but I don't mean abandonment like that.

They find the door locked & keep ringing the doorbell. *Go away,* I holler through the mail slot. *Sunday dinners are all over.*

They can't believe it; not even my daughter who told me about story plots in the first place. They think I'll wait around for them to abandon me. No way. I'm leaving them first.

There's a pay phone at the corner. After they leave my phone starts ringing over & over until I yank the jack out of the wall.

It is quiet. I go through my recipe box & throw out all their favourites. There's nothing left. I wonder what I'll eat. Maybe I'll keep trying different foods at the neighbourhood diner until I discover some favourites of my own.

This is my story. Not much more can happen.

•

Chicken Wings

•

•

I've got this man, Barb tells me. *He's all right. If you want him you can have him.* I did her a favour once, & she keeps trying to repay it.

Barb asks the waitress for some fancy imported beer, but this place only stocks Labatt's & Molson's. Barb acts surprised, as though she can hardly believe it, as though we don't come here every week. Me, I just want a light beer & want it now. I get thirsty listening to Barb & the way she carries on. The waitress wants to take our chicken order but we're not in any rush.

What's the matter with him? I ask.

Nothing. There's just no chemistry. Anyway, I like them younger.

Don't we all, I think, remembering some young guys I've known in the past. Not lately though, so I ask, *Just how ancient is this geezer anyway?*

I'm forty-eight & Barb's forty-five, but we pass for younger. We can do it. We dye our hair & keep up-to-date on fashion. It makes a difference. I look at women who don't do this & have no idea who they are. I don't know what goes on inside their minds. I wonder if they're old everywhere, or only where it shows. Like their brain: does it forget things & reminisce about the old days? Or does it know the world still spins & new things happen?

It turns out this guy is fifty-three, the kind of age difference that's okay for other people, not necessarily me.

The waitress brings the beer. I notice mine's not light but I don't care. I'm so thirsty my throat is swollen.

Barb says, *Hey, my friend here ordered a light.*

I don't care, I say. *I'm so thirsty I'm going to keep it.*

Barb gives me her same old lecture about people walking on me like a door-mat. She's taken assertiveness training & it shows.

He looks older though, Barb says. *We only went out a couple of times. I forgot to mention his hair is almost white. Last week I saw our reflection in a store window. I suddenly realized I was walking along the street with a white-haired man, in broad daylight where everyone could see me.*

Barb shakes salt in her beer while she's talking; I always think this looks stupid.

But he's okay, she goes on. *You two might hit it off. I think you like them a little bit older. Whatta you say? It won't hurt you just to meet him.*

I can't believe this conversation. Women don't talk like this, except cheerleaders in old Gidget movies. Perhaps teenage girls swap boyfriends, being so slick about it that the boys never know what happened. Maybe the boys even think they're responsible & feel little pangs of guilt.

The waitress keeps coming by, so we place our order. Barb wants a different dressing on the salad. *The house dressing's pretty nice,* the waitress tells her. We already know this, from coming here each week. Barb agrees to try it, as though she's doing her a favour.

What's his name? I ask, & Barb tells me. I try to imagine introducing a guy named Floyd to my family & friends. *It's an awfully funny name,* I complain. *Wasn't that the barber on the old Andy Griffiths Show?*

I can see I've hurt Barb's feelings. She's already been out with this guy, despite his name.

I've gone out with names that sounded better, I insist, but she mentions that I've also gone out with worse. I shouldn't tell her anything. I always regret it later. She has a 20/20 memory.

He's getting over a marriage break-up, she says.

Sure, I say. *Who isn't? Last Christmas I sent twice as many cards because all the couples I know have broken up.*

You know anyone who's still married? Barb asks, & I say, *Yeah. A guy in accounting. He & his wife are into zinnias. They'd better not split up. They'll never find anyone else who cares about flowers that much.*

Zinnias? Are they the stiff ones?

Yeah. They look like they've been dried up & preserved already.

I like zinnia colours, Barb says. *They're nice in autumn.*

Yeah, but this couple is seriously into zinnias. They win prizes at flower shows.

Then I remember someone else, & tell her, *Also one of my brothers.*

One brother what? Grows zinnias?

No. One of my brothers is still married. Tony. The vegetarian. The one whose wife does yoga.

No kids, though, Barb says, as though this explains it, & probably it does.

Barb wants another job. They brought a young guy in last summer & already he's above her. She fiddles with a chicken wing & wonders what to do.

Don't rock the boat, I say. *Not till you've got something else lined up. Geez, it's not that easy to find a job these days.* What I also mean is, not at our age, but I don't say it. I was out of work almost a year before landing the job I've got.

I ought to get an extra sauce for my mother, I say. *She loves this stuff. It's probably addictive. Maybe it's the salt.*

Look at all these old people, Barb says. *They shouldn't be eating salt. It'll make their blood pressure go up.*

I look around & see nothing but old folks, or else families with lots of noisy little kids. Kids get a special menu that folds into a party hat. Suddenly I realize Barb & I are social misfits. *We don't belong here,* I say. *Next week let's try some place else.*

But they make great chicken wings, Barb objects. She says if only she had that recipe she'd cook her own chicken & save lots of money.

Yeah, right! I say, being sarcastic, because she hates cooking. I hate it too. I say, *The trouble with men is they always want to eat. They expect a meal every single night, & extra ones on weekends.*

Just like kids, Barb says, & then we ask about each other's kids. They're into serious relationships already. Barb & I feel a little jealous, but anyway, that's life.

We wonder if we should go crazy & have hot apple pie, but finally decide our waistlines are more important.

I ask, *Do you really think I'd like this guy?* & then confess, *The trouble is, I only like men that I can't have. As soon as a guy shows a bit of interest, I don't want him any more. It's like I panic & back off.*

Barb says. *What DO you want? Someone who doesn't like you? I give up.*

How's your mom? I ask, changing the subject.

Her mother's all right, just getting older. These days when she gets sick it takes her longer to get better. But her mom's still okay on her own, & so is mine. We worry a lot these days about what will happen when they aren't.

Lately Barb & I keep worrying that we're turning into our mothers. It seems weird because they've always been so old. My mother's always been seventy. When I was a little kid I thought she was ancient, & in high school I thought the same thing. Now it's thirty years later & I'm still thinking it. Momma started out so old she never gets any older. My kids see me the same way. It makes me mad.

So, what about it? Barb asks. *Do you want to meet Floyd or not? He's working late tonight at the plaza. We could drop by & say hello.*

I don't know if I feel like it. This is how I decide to handle it, knowing I'll finally give in but not wanting to seem eager. So then I say, *We've already seen the movie at the Roxy. Sure. I guess so. Why not?*

I'm looking around for the waitress, hoping she'll notice & she does. *We need more coffee over here,* I tell her. She forgets the cream, but comes back when I yell, *Hey!*

How about that? I say to Barb. *I'm getting assertive. Aren't you impressed?* But she's not paying any attention. She's got her eye on a guy at the bar.

•

The King & Queen

•

•

MARTHA IS LOOKING FOR HENRY MOORE, although he is dead, although she knows this & believes it, meaning in her mind but not her gut.

She comes from Toronto where the art gallery keeps its collection of Moore sculptures in a separate room which is hushed like a cathedral. The great brooding stones are bathed in light which filters down from skylights & creates shadowy images on the polished floor. The air is fresh & invigorating, smelling of ozone & green fields. Martha goes there whenever she needs to & always leaves feeling revitalized.

Years ago, in the hallway outside the gallery, Martha saw photographs of Moore bronzes outdoors in Britain. She suddenly realized the massive sculptures belonged outside. These women were self-sufficient. They didn't need other women around them, & wouldn't want them. From then on, whenever she gazed at the sculptures, she imagined them in an outdoor setting, resting on green grass, surrounded by rolling landscape, the terrain they had emerged from. Curved shoulders & thighs slowly arose from the earth, until the women reclined on the ground, looking around, undisturbed by their surroundings. Women who are wise, serene, able to cope with anything.

Martha would like to be capable herself.

One day the photographs were gone. *Maybe in storage,* a guard suggested, but they never reappeared. It hardly mattered. Martha's retinas retained them. Whenever she walks along that hallway she still sees them.

Now she is travelling to Britain to search for the sculptures she saw in those photographs. She needs to see Moore's bronzes outside, against the lush green background that only exists in a wet country.

Her friends & family said she was crazy, couldn't afford to take the time off work, couldn't afford the airfare in the first place. Martha nodded, said they were right. As if she cared. She'd already bought the ticket anyway.

Beyond the train window, all the way from Gatwick to London, the landscape of those photographs surrounds her. She feels she's doing what she had to, that there'd never been a choice. She's travelling toward the only kind of history that really matters to her life.

Travellers come to Britain looking for other stones. They have been making these pilgrimages for years, one generation after another. Stonehenge & Avebury. Chalk cliffs. Elgin marbles in the British Museum. Tombstones of ancestors in quiet country churchyards. Martha's family has solid English roots & can understand this. They prepared lists of cathedrals & museums, favourite walking tours of London. *& of course the changing of the guard. You won't miss that.* Martha certainly intends to.

She writes postcards: *So this is jet lag. So this is England,* then consults her address book to remember who she knows back home.

Once Martha prepared a book list for a conference on stress. She didn't bother reading the books, just their jackets & tables of contents. She checked the writing style, noticing jargon: *burned-out, stressed-out,* words that now apply to her.

She stares at Moores inside buildings, one gallery after another, but that's not why she came. She can do that in Toronto. So she studies guidebooks & maps, preparing to search the countryside, almost as though she knows what she is doing, as though she knows who she is & why she does this.

She has a BritRail pass & travels wherever she wants, zigzagging back & forth: Leeds, Edinburgh, Norwich, Moore's home in Hertfordshire. Time after time, in one B & B after another, kindly people say, *You can't miss the turnoff. Walk west half & mile or so, then there's a road off to the left. You can't miss it.* Martha always could.

The women are beautiful & strong, rounded, but rooted solidly to the ground. Each woman alone with nature. Martha can approach them, move around, explore them from every direction. She knows it might take her a lifetime to understand each one. She returns to the same pieces again & again for warmth & comfort. *We survived,* they seem to tell her, *We will continue to survive. You will too.*

They understand about the baby who died inside her.

The landscape soothes her too. She feels at home. The soft rolling hillsides seem to remind her of some earlier time, inside her mother's womb perhaps.

She is finally able to return home.

The day before her departure she hears of Moore's King & Queen, privately owned by someone in Scotland. She's not familiar with this work at all. Even though she's only been interested in the massive reclining women, now that she hears of this sculpture she wants to see it. She looks for Dumfries on the map. It looks accessible, north from Carlisle, not far from the border.

She is able to change her ticket & wires her family not to expect her. She doesn't explain. Anyway what could she say that would make sense? She doesn't notify the people she works for. When she doesn't show up on Monday morning they'll be surprised.

Now Martha's in Scotland. At the train station in Dumfries she climbs inside a taxi & asks how much it will cost to get to Moore's King & Queen. The cabbie doesn't know what she's talking about. No one else does either, not the other cabbies in the queue, not the stationmaster. The information kiosk & the art gallery are closed because of Good Friday. She had forgotten all about Easter.

Two potters in a studio tell how they found the sculpture by accident, driving miles from town on an errand, suddenly looking up & discovering the figures silhouetted on a hillside. They could hardly believe it. They get out their ordinance maps to show the cabbie how to get there.

They seem to drive forever, through a light rain, along narrow winding country roads, past mossy hillsides dotted with sheep. They are no pedestrians, but once a car swerves around a blind curve toward them. Martha holds her breath when this happens, as though this trip is full of hazard.

Finally, there they are. A king, a queen. Silhouetted on a hilltop, against the misty louring sky.

Don't leave, she tells the cabdriver. *Wait for me. I'll be a while.*

There are no laws against trespassing here, so Martha is free to climb the wet slippery hillside, past sheep which are scattered along the hillside like outcroppings of rock. The animals ignore her. She thinks they are probably accustomed to strangers. She imagines other people like herself driving these winding roads, opening the gate, climbing this slope toward the sculpture.

She climbs, watching the king & queen gradually increase in size. It is snowing a little now & the ground is muddy. Finally she stands in front of them.

They are not what she'd imagined, not at all like the solid women reclining on the ground. Coming here has been a waste of time.

Martha tries to pay attention to them, but thoughts keep nagging against her brain: It will be difficult to climb back down the slippery hill. She should do it soon. It's already late afternoon. She is trespassing, doesn't belong here. She doesn't like being on someone's property, whether it's legal or not. She'll click her camera once or twice to prove she really made it, & then head back.

Her feet are wet & cold. She needs to keep walking, so she wanders around the figures, exploring every angle of their bony outlines. She finally touches their cool green feet. Their expressions never change. They have seen too much already to be startled by this woman.

Their heads are far above her, staring into the distance. Martha wants to holler, *Look at me. Pay attention. I've come all the way from Canada, searched through a town where no one had heard of you, hired a cab to drive all the way out here, climbed this muddy hill. My feet are freezing. I'll probably get pneumonia…*

She thinks this will make a good story when she gets home. Her friends will laugh & remind her, *We told you not to go.*

The king & queen sit side by side on a bench, not touching, looking straight ahead. The queen holds her hands together in her lap. Their robes are simple, & their feet bare. Their bodies are narrow & spare, their shoulders sloped, as though worn down by time. The shape of the king's head suggests a beard, a crown. Their skin is green now, their proud features softened by weather.

They are all alone. Luckily they have each other. They look as if they've been here forever, these ancient rulers, century after century. The world around them changes but they are constant. They can't simply lie down & die. They are here because people need them.

Martha follows their eyes, stares at hills & water. A pond. The hills beyond. One house. An empty road. Perhaps this is a bronze king's & queen's idea of heaven.

They remain. It doesn't matter whether the sun shines, whether snow or rain falls. This is a view they keep watching anyway. This is as permanent as anything gets.

It is enough.

•

Vampire Kisses

•

•

THIS IS A STORY ABOUT EDDA & A VAMPIRE, if you believe in vampires, dear reader, & even if you don't.

Edda kisses a vampire whenever she wants to. Other nights she wears a garlic necklace & places a cross beneath her pillow in easy reach. But she never needs it; the vampire always shows up at the right time.

Whenever Edda menstruates, the vampire comes & sucks her blood. Edda lets him. It is so much easier than tampons or rags or pads. Anyway, she likes it.

Edda tells him vampire stories. *Long ago in Salem,* she says, *women were burned at the stake as witches for knowing vampires. Knowing them in the biblical sense, that is,* she adds, & giggles.

The vampire remembers this, & tells her stories of stakes plunged into innocent hearts, of beheadings, burning corpses. *Superstition, that's all it was,* the vampire says & laughs.

Bats swoop around his head. They echo his laugh in high-pitched squeaks. Edda knows there is more to their laughter than she can hear; on higher levels beyond her perception the bat sounds go on & on.

Edda's lover lies in bed beside her & sleeps soundly. He never notices vampire movement beneath the bedclothes, never hears the stories Edda & the vampire tell each other. Bat squeaks never disturb his sleep.

Every month the full moon sails through the sky & Edda menstruates. The vampire slides beneath her patchwork quilt, flowered sheets, flannelette nightgown. The vampire sucks her menstrual blood, abandoned eggs, unfertilized babies. Edda has one orgasm after another as he does this.

This happens every full moon until one month the vampire arrives & Edda's not bleeding. *I've got the flu,* she tells him. *I throw up a lot. You'd better stay away so you don't catch it.*

The vampire can hardly believe it. *How could you do this to me?* he asks. *Don't you two use birth control? How could you let yourself get pregnant?*

Oh no! How could this happen? asks weepy Edda.

No one is happy. Not the vampire without blood to suck. Not Edda who throws up every morning, feels bloated & grumpy all day, thrashes about irritably at night. Not her lover. Sometimes Edda's arm swats against him & wakes him up; he moves farther & farther toward his edge of the bed.

Edda tells her lover nothing. He doesn't know about the vampire or the pregnancy & thinks Edda is changing into some other person. She's no longer the sweet young damsel he'd fancied himself in love with. His eyes are starting to stray elsewhere. He would leave Edda's bed but hates to hear women weep & scream, hates to have them throw temper tantrums & aim dishes & dictionaries at his head.

This is the situation, dear reader. How would you solve it?

Well, it depends upon your reverence for life & abhorrence of abortion. It depends on whether you believe in vampires or not.

Edda can't wait while you procrastinate. She gets more & more depressed & finally tosses herself off a balcony into the flowerbed below. She doesn't die like she expects to, but loses the baby. At first she's sad about both these things, but gradually adjusts.

The vampire resumes his monthly vigils beneath the bedclothes.

The lover decides Edda is the same sweet damsel he'd been in love with after all. He never looks at another woman again, or at least not for quite a while.

& Edda? *Sorry Edda,* says the doctor. *you'll never be able to conceive again. Goshdarn,* says Edda, & forces a couple of tears from her eyes. She keeps an onion in her pocket so she can do this whenever she needs to.

So everyone is happy. Life goes on, pretty much as before. Stories like this are always so reassuring.

•

Looking for World War II

•

•

I saw a submarine once in Lake Ontario. Lorna says this to get attention.

Usually she tells them nothing personal, these people she sits & gabs with on Friday evenings. Instead she tries to think up wise-crack remarks to entertain the regulars at the window table of the local pub. *Good old Lorna,* she imagines them saying after she finishes her second *Labatt's* & leaves. *Good old Lorna. She never changes. Always good for a laugh.*

Tonight the guys are talking about Camp X. Gord is fascinated by World War II, the romance, the intrigue & espionage. He was almost old enough to enlist when the war suddenly ended. He still resents this. *I drove around Whitby for hours last weekend,* he says, *trying to find Camp X. There's just a plaque & a wind sock in an empty field where it used to be. Dammit. If this was the U S of A, there'd be a whole museum, glass cabinets with secret documents, pictures of frogmen on the walls, tours through the tunnels …*

& a Golden Arches across the street, Bill says. *Be thankful.*

So Lorna tells them about the sub.

Dammit, says Gord. *In all the years I've known you, how come you never mentioned the sub?*

They believe her. At the time no one believed her except the girlfriend who saw it too. When Lorna went home & told her parents they said, *Stop being silly,* & that was that. Now she wonders, did she really tell them? Would she expect them to believe her? A submarine was so unlikely. Probably she told no one.

When? asks Charlie.

When what?

When did you see it?

I don't know exactly. I was a kid, about ten years old maybe, at the most. That'd make it '44 or '45. There is silence around the table as the others subtract forty-five from the current year & then add ten.

That's amazing, says Charlie. *I'd heard that German subs came down the St. Lawrence but I've never talked to anyone who actually saw one.*

Lorna's no longer sure she saw a sub. Their belief has unnerved her. *It wasn't a sub exactly,* she backtracks, *just a periscope, sticking up maybe a foot above the water.*

A periscope? Bill whistles softly. *Really? Wow!*

When I went home & told my parents they said it must have been a stick.

Jesus, says Charlie. *A stick. Floating upright in the water. Give me a break.*

They did say that, she remembers. They were her parents. She tried to believe them.

Lorna wonders whether a kid of ten years old can be sure of anything. War & childhood are fuzzy ideas to grab hold of. She wonders whether any of her childhood memories can possibly be true. Perhaps she can't imagine what it was like to be that child any better than she can imagine being someone else ... her parents, or her girlfriend, or a sailor in the freezing North Atlantic, like her cousin.

There was barbed wire around the water works in those days, Lorna says, *in case the water supply might be an enemy target, & searchlights, & a sentry box at the entrance. It was spooky.*

It's easier to imagine the sub, says Gord. *I've heard that German subs kept an eye on what was happening. I believe it.*

My girlfriend & I collected things for the war effort. Lorna continues. *We gathered up everything, cans, newspapers, tin foil from packages of cigarettes ...*

Charlie interrupts, *They didn't use any of that stuff. The government just wanted people to feel involved. It was just for morale. I read it somewhere.*

Lorna ignores him. *We had to bring things to school to fill up ditty bags for sailors. Canned goods & cigarettes.*

Marybeth finally speaks. *Ditty bags? What's that?*

Some kind of kit bags sailors keep odds & ends in. We had to write letters to sailors for homework. After they were marked we put them inside ditty bags & waited, hoping for an answer.

Really! Marybeth says. *Can you imagine kids today being so naive? Thinking some sailor might write them back?*

I knew a girl who got a letter, Lorna says. *The rest of us were jealous. My girlfriend & I wrote extra letters & sneaked them into the ditty bags at noon hour. We were sure someone would send an answer. Who knows what kids like that could see in Lake Ontario if they wanted?*

Don't be silly, Bill assures her. *You saw a sub. A boy might have dreamed up a submarine just from wanting to see one, but it wouldn't have entered a girl's head.*

Thank God we're liberated now, Lorna says. *Little girls can dream of subs & guns & war just like the boys. Ain't progress grand?*

I never allowed my son to play with guns, Marybeth says.

What about your daughters? Lorna asks. *They're more likely to need them.*

Ten years old. The man from the next apartment grabbed her on the landing & held her tight against the wall. He was hard & bumpy & smelled like ashtrays of old cigar butts. A door opened along the hall & he let her go. Did she tell her parents about this? What words would she have used? Perhaps this was the beginning of secrets.

I want to go back to Whitby on a weekday when it's quiet, Gord is saying. *I went on a Saturday. Kids were riding trail bikes back & forth, & two guys were flying model planes. All those engines roaring & spluttering. It was like a sound track for a movie about the war.*

Lorna's sailor cousin was ten years older & she'd always followed him around like a puppy. When she was small she rode on his shoulders, later on the handlebars of his bike. One day when he was home on leave they were alone at someone's cottage. She couldn't swim, so she grabbed him tight around the neck & he swam out to a sandbar. His hair felt soft against her cheek. Water splashed up into her face & blurred her vision. She wanted to rub her eyes but didn't dare take a hand away from his neck. When they reached the sandbar she stood & watched him swim back & forth. She remembers her amazement at how smoothly he could do this, how she stood in shallow water with hot sunshine all around her & thought the world was perfect. Then he swam back to shore & left her.

She called & waved but he didn't look back. She watched him open the cottage door & disappear into the darkness of the screened porch. Maybe he sat there & watched her; maybe not.

He's playing some kind of joke, she thought, & later she'd have to pretend that it was funny. She couldn't swim. She stood in water half-way up her thighs, too deep to sit down, afraid to move for fear she'd step off the sandbar & drown. She waited, getting more & more frantic. Perhaps he was packing up, would go back to his navy base & leave her stranded forever.

Lorna wonders now whether the sandbar even existed, whether her cousin just told her she was standing on one & she believed him. Perhaps the lake was shallow a long way out & she hadn't known.

How long did she have to wait until he returned & saved her? Five minutes? An hour? She has no way of knowing. When he finally came to get her she couldn't speak. She just held him, held him, held him, while he laughed. She clung tight to his neck all the way back to shore & still could not let go. He tried to put her down but she held on tighter. He finally lay down with her on a couch & held her while she cried herself to sleep.

If he was alive, if he walked into this pub right now, she would hold him like that again.

Charlie is asking Marybeth if she's ever read *A Man Called Intrepid.*

I'm not interested in the past, she tells him. *It's so irrelevant.*

Don't be stupid, Lorna says. *It mattered. People died, & the ones who didn't were changed forever. I had a cousin in that war. He died at sea.*

A few drops of beer remain in her glass. Lorna tips her head back & tries to drain them. *Anyway,* she says, *War's fun but I've got to run.* She grabs her jacket & heads for the washroom.

Lorna watches someone in a mirror who puts on lipstick, who runs a comb through hennaed hair that needs touching up, who puts on Lorna's navy pea jacket & buttons it up. The woman in the mirror is a stranger. She is older than Lorna. She is plain & uninteresting & has no stories that matter. Lorna leaves her in the bathroom.

As she makes her way between tables she hears Marybeth say, *That Lorna. She's getting weird.*

I heard that. Lorna stands in the doorway, feet wide apart. She holds an imaginary pistol with both hands & points it at Marybeth. *Pow,* Lorna says, *right between the eyes.* Then she goes out, quietly closing the door behind her.

The evening feels soft around her. A breeze blows a plastic bag along the gutter. It makes a shushing sound. Miles away, beside a lake, long grass is swaying. A sliver of moon slices through cloud. Below a bluff, at the shoreline, something moves. Perhaps it is human.

•

Fundamentals

•

•

SHARON FIDDLES WITH DIALS that don't work anyway: heater, air vent, radio. Fields fly past the window. *Oats*, Daddy says, *red clover*. As if it matters.

I could read to Momma, make her cups of tea ...

Daddy slows down for a turn. Sharon watches his feet slide up & down: clutch, then brake, clutch again, step on the gas. Four more years till she's sixteen & can get a learner's permit. When the time comes she will be ready.

No. The doctor said absolute quiet. It's just till school starts. Only a month. Then the car wobbles. *Goddam potholes*, Daddy keeps muttering as Sharon watches how to fix a flat. *We could turn around & go back*, she suggests.

When Aunt Addie & Uncle Clarence visit at Christmas Uncle Clarence always says a long prayer before anyone can eat, then Daddy jokes that the food is cold before he stops. But Sharon has never been to their place, never seen this town with old brick houses & big front lawns. Sharon thinks of home, the neat little shrubs, friendly look-alike houses. *Look*, she says, *they have three floors*.

Yeah. Just the two of them rattling around inside there. What a waste.

The screen door opens. Aunt Addie beckons them inside, but Daddy calls, *No, I've got to get right back.*

Not even a cup of tea? A piece of cinnamon cake?

I'd better not. I don't like being away so long. He hugs Sharon & is gone. A cloud of dust wraps around the car as he drives away.

Finally Sharon looks around. Rows of flowers lead to the porch: clumps of blue & pink & yellow. Bees are buzzing around the blossoms, the air silent except for that sleepy humming sound. *You look hot,* Aunt Addie says. *Let's get some lemonade.*

Through a dark hallway, then up steep stairs, into a guest room with flowered wallpaper & a patchwork quilt. Old photographs hang on the walls. Aunt Addie points at a teenager on a porch swing. *That's your mother when she was young. This was going to be our little girl's room. We could pretend you're her.*

I already have a momma & daddy, Sharon says.

Aunt Addie keeps a pitcher of lemonade in the refrigerator. It's cold enough, but she adds ice-cubes anyway. Then they sit on the verandah, hidden behind dappled vine leaves. Ice clinks inside their glasses while they watch whatever happens. Aunt Addie tells about the neighbours. *That woman with the stroller, one day her husband just cleared out their bank account & disappeared. She moved back here with her parents. God tests us in his fire until we're strong. See that man cutting his lawn? He hangs out laundry. I don't know what his wife does. I never see her.*

Maybe she has to rest like Momma.

Maybe drinking is more like it. No drunkards in our family, praise the Lord.

A car drives past, its windows open, music floating around it. *I know that song,* says Sharon. *It's called Runaway. I like the way it goes up high & then back down, that wa-wa-wa sound.*

Satan hides messages inside that kind of music. I'll have to tell your Momma you've been listening. I'm sorry, but I have to do it for your own good. Sharon thinks Aunt Addie must be crazy. Her mother loves that song. She sings wa-wa-wa while Daddy laughs & taps his feet.

Sharon looks at rows of growing vegetables. *Wow! You don't need to buy food at a store.* Aunt Addie shows how to pull up carrots & radishes, how to pick the outside leaves of lettuce so new ones keep growing up. *These onions are awfully small,* Sharon says, then watches Aunt Addie dip them in salt & eat them raw.

Sharon dips pieces of liver in a dish of flour, then Aunt Addie drops them in a hot pan. *Yuck! I don't eat liver,* Sharon mentions. *You do now,* Aunt Addie says.

Uncle Clarence comes home & calls her Rose of Sharon. *Just Sharon,* she reminds him, but he says, *No. Rose of Sharon. It's from the Bible.* Before supper he asks God's blessing. *We'll keep this young girl inside our Christian home. We'll suffer her like Jesus suffered little children.*

Sharon interrupts. *Tell God I want to go home.*

She's willful, Lord, & doesn't know about your mercy. We'll lead her toward your shining light. Afterward his face is purple. *Never do that again,* he hollers, *I was talking to the Lord! Don't ever interrupt our conversation!*

I want to go home.

God wants you right here. Whatever God decides is what you do.

Sharon lies in bed, her transistor radio beneath the pillow, the earplug in her ear. While the Shirelles are singing *Soldier Boy* she starts to cry.

In the morning Aunt Addie gets ready to go shopping. *Put a dress on*, she says.

I didn't bring one.

Heaven's sake, child, you can't go downtown wearing pants.

They're jeans.

Pants are for men. Women wear dresses.

So Sharon stays home & watches out the bedroom window, her transistor radio in her hand. She dances to whatever tune begins to play. *Monday, Monday*, she sings. *Can't trust that day.* When she sees Aunt Addie heading up the street Sharon hides the radio beneath the cotton tick.

They unpack parcels. Flowered fabric that looks like wallpaper. An envelope of tissue paper pieces. Aunt Addie unfolds fabric on the kitchen table & pins tissue paper on top, then starts cutting. Sharon fastens edges together with pins. Aunt Addie shoves her knee against the treadle & her machine sews the fabric into dresses for Sharon to try on. Sharon spins around & feels a rustling against her legs. *They're beautiful*, Sharon says. *I look so pretty, like a pioneer girl.*

Pride is a sin, Aunt Addie reminds her.

Now Sharon wears pretty dresses & helps around the house. There's nothing else to do so she might as well. She picks tomatoes & leaf lettuce, pulls beans off a vine & strips the strings off, slits pea-pods open & fills the cooking pot with peas. Every night they make something different. Sharon pays attention; if she learns how to cook maybe she can go home & look after her mother.

Sunday morning they go to a church in a room with ordinary windows instead of coloured pictures. They sit on folding chairs. A voice shouts, *Praise the Lord*. Sharon waits for someone to shush that person up, but no one does. Then Uncle Clarence shouts it too. Soon Sharon gets used to it.

Amazing Grace reminds Sharon of *Runaway*, how voices go off from the rest of the tune. She can't get that hymn out of her mind & hums it all the time. She sees Aunt Addie & Uncle Clarence smile whenever they hear her. Sometimes that's why she hums it, so they will love her like the little girl they never had.

Sharon writes a letter to her mother. *Is my name really Rose of Sharon?* Her mother seems very far away. Sharon looks at the teenager on the bedroom wall & doesn't recognize her at all. *Send me a picture of you & Daddy*, she adds.

Uncle Clarence makes Sharon read aloud from his Bible: *I am the rose of Sharon, and the lily of the valleys*. Every morning he assigns a verse to memorize & she recites it at supper-time. At first the verses are short: *Remember now thy creator in the days of thy youth. Seek ye the Lord while he may be found*. Sharon says longer ones over & over until she remembers: *Rachel envied her sister; and said unto Jacob, Give me children, or else I die.*

Uncle Clarence wants Sharon to learn one book of the Bible really well & picks The Song of Solomon. Each evening she reads a chapter & he tells which verse to memorize. Aunt Addie knits in the parlour until the lesson is over & then brings out lemonade. They sit on the porch swing while ice clinks in their glasses & evening descends.

One day a lady visits & brings her daughter. *Your hair is too short*, Josephine complains. *Short hair is for boys.*

What grade are you in? Sharon asks her. *What kind of music do you like?*

Are you saved? Josephine asks.

In the evening Sharon reads, *Comfort me with apples, for I am sick of love. His left hand is under my head, and his right hand doth embrace me*. Uncle Clarence says, *Your Momma & Daddy will be amazed. You'll be able to witness to them about the Good Book*. Sharon keeps reading; it is easier to read than talk. But Uncle Clarence interrupts. *My dream is for you to be saved. I don't want you to leave until it happens. Memorize verse 16*. Sharon looks at it, *My beloved is mine, and I am his: he feedeth among the lilies*. It is a short verse, & easy.

People witness every Sunday. Bad things kept happening before they found the Lord. They were sinners until they found God & got strong. Now they want to tell everyone about it.

Josephine witnesses to Sharon whenever she gets the chance. *I need to practise. Lots of heathens go to my school. I want to gather them in for God.*

It sounds like rounding up cows, Sharon says, *like in a western movie.*

You've seen a movie? Josephine asks. *Only heathens go to movies. But don't worry. I'm going to save you.*

Sharon sings *Amazing Grace* as she helps Aunt Addie in the garden, *How sweet the sound that saved a wretch like me* ... She pretends this song was written for her, that she's a wretch, whatever that is. *I once was lost* ... It's easy to imagine she's lost. She IS lost, or else her parents are. Why don't they come & get her? Why don't they hurry up? She's beginning to forget her real name. *Was blind, but now I see*. Sharon imagines being blind. She squeezes her eyes shut & is lost inside eternal darkness. The world is black, but she gets used to it. Then Sharon opens her eyes & is dazzled by the glory of God. The chorus happens over & over. *Amazing grace, how sweet the sound* ... She remembers Jackie Gleason said that on TV, *How sweet it is.*

Do you believe yet? Uncle Clarence asks. *Are you saved yet?* asks Josephine.

Every Sunday Sharon listens to voices reaching up toward God.

God sits high up on the church beams, feet dangling, head tilted to one side to hear the singing better, fingers tip-tapping to the music. He wears a happy smile.

When we've been there ten thousand years, bright shining as the sun, we've no less days to sing God's praise than when we first begun. Sharon tries to figure this out, but then the chorus begins again & she forgets arithmetic.

A letter from Momma contains a snapshot: all three of them together: Momma, Daddy, Sharon. *No,* Momma writes. *Clarence is wrong. Your name is simply Sharon.*

Time for Bible reading, Uncle Clarence calls.

Not now, Sharon says. *We're making meat loaf.*

The Lord is more important.

It's all right, says Aunt Addie. *I'll show you another day.*

Let my beloved come into his garden, and eat his pleasant fruits, Sharon reads. *We bought blueberries today,* she says. *We're having them for supper.*

The phone rings, It's Sharon's father calling long distance to say the baby's dead. *What baby?* Sharon asks.

I thought you understood. That's why your momma had to stay in bed. To try to save the baby.

You never told me anything about it, Sharon accuses. She can hardly believe it. There's been a baby in her family & she hadn't even known. Now that baby's already dead. *Was it a girl or boy?* she asks, but Daddy says he doesn't know. Sharon is sure he must be lying. It is sinful to tell a lie. *It wasn't big enough to live,* he says.

I want to come home now, Sharon tells him.

Not yet. Your momma's still awfully weak. Let me speak to Addie a minute.

Sharon throws herself down on the bed & starts crying for a tiny baby who will never do anything. She cries about her father & mother who tell her nothing. Mostly she cries for herself.

Uncle Clarence sits down on the edge of the bed. His hand is soft upon her head. *You have to accept it,* he says. *It's all part of God's great plan.*

It doesn't make sense. I always wanted a baby brother or sister.

I know. Your aunt & I always wanted a baby too, but the Lord keeps saying no. Angels push your baby back & forth in a heavenly stroller. They sing lullabies & strum on harps. Can you imagine that?

No.

Neither can I, he admits. *We'd have named her Rose of Sharon.* His voice hums like far-off insects. He lies down on the bed & holds her until she falls asleep.

God killed the baby on purpose, Josephine explains. *He was trying to reach you.*

God's stupid then, yells Sharon. *He isn't fair!* Josephine looks scared & runs down the stairs, but Sharon races after her, yelling, *He's stupid! He isn't fair!* She hollers, *I hate him!* out the front door as she watches Josephine run down the street.

Aunt Addie grabs her. *What's going on? Josephine ran past me like a scalded cat.*

I hate God! Sharon shouts.

Aunt Addie drops down on her knees pulling Sharon with her. *Forgive her, Lord,* she begs over & over. *She's just a child &*

doesn't understand what she's saying. Don't smite her with your wrath. She opens her eyes & glares at Sharon. *Pray!* she hisses. *Holler it out. Beg for forgiveness.*

Sharon yells, *I never even got to see the baby,* & then starts sobbing, *Josephine's wrong. It's not my fault.*

Aunt Addie prays frantically. *Listen to her, Lord. She's crying penitential tears.*

Sharon starts to get up to get a kleenex but Aunt Addie yanks her down again & keeps praying. *Forgive her Lord. She's just a child.* God is silent. He doesn't smash the house with a thunderbolt or set it on fire with lightning.

Afterward Aunt Addie says, *Of course it's not your fault. Don't be silly.*

Josephine says God made Momma go to bed so I'd come here & get saved.

Oh dear. Some people think God plans everything. Clarence thinks that way too. Sometimes we can't imagine why things happen. Why'd your mother's baby die? Why didn't I ever have one? If we believe there's a good reason it's easier to stand it.

Does God do that? Is it true?

Nobody really knows. You know, I didn't like Clarence's church at first. I was an Anglican like your mother & liked my religion more secretive & peaceful. But I've been going there a long time now. I don't ask questions.

Are you saved?

Well, one day I went to the front of the church & said I loved Jesus. I don't think that makes me saved, but if it does, then I guess I am. Anyway, don't worry about religion yet. You're only twelve years old. Right now let's make rhubarb cobbler.

After Aunt Addie leaves for Ladies' Aid, Sharon opens the Bible & reads, *How beautiful are thy feet with shoes, O princes' daughter.*

Sit up on my lap to read it, Uncle Clarence suggests.

I'm too big to sit on someone's knee.

No you're not. Do what I tell you. There now. That feels good. Start reading again. He is holding her tight.

Sharon reads, *The joints of thy thighs are like jewels...* & then looks up. Aunt Addie stands in the doorway. *Hi,* Sharon says. *You got home early,* & then starts over, *The joints of thy thighs are like jewels ...*

No, says Uncle Clarence. *That's enough. Run along now.*

Aunt Addie buys a basket of peaches for Sharon to take home to Momma. *I want Red Havens,* Sharon says. *They're easy to peel & the pits fall out. This time last year I didn't know the difference.*

Slice them up at the last minute & add sugar so they don't turn brown.

How did you learn all this in the first place? Sharon asks.

I can't remember. Maybe my Aunt Clara told me.

Sharon thinks about that little niece growing up & then telling her own niece. It could go on & on, she thinks, like the begats in Uncle Clarence's Bible.

When Sharon leaves Aunt Addie dabs a handkerchief against her eyes & says, *I'm going to miss you, child. I won't forget this summer.* Sharon says, *Me too,* to be polite, then suddenly realizes it might be true.

•

Acknowledgments

The quote on page 46 is from Dorothy Parker, 'Resumé,' *The Portable Dorothy Parker*, permission courtesy of Penguin Books, 1976.

The quote on page 72 is from Emily Dickinson, *The Complete Poems of Emily Dickinson*, Little Brown, 1960.

The quote on page 76 is from Emily Carr, taken from a letter to *The Vancouver Province* (April, 1912), mentioned in *Emily Carr in France*, by Ian M. Thom, Vancouver Art Gallery, 1991.

The quote on page 80 is from Robert Louis Stevenson, *A Child's Garden of Verses*.

Thanks to Kristin Andrychuk, Helen Humphreys, Ted Plantos & The Ontario Arts Council Writers' Reserve Program.

•

Credits

Pencils:
Paragraph, 12,3,1990
Intersections '92, Writings by City College Instructors,
George Brown College
City College News, 10,3,93, George Brown College

Somewhere a Piper Plays Elephant Songs:
Event, 22,3,1993-1994

Bellefair:
Event, 22,3,1993-1994

Annabel as the Universe Unfolds around Her:
New Quarterly, 14,3,1994

The Mating Dance of the Blue-Footed Booby:
Descant 78, 3,3,1992

Maude:
Vivid, Stories by Five Women, Mercury Press, 1989

Fractals:
The MacGuffin, 10,2,1994

Vampire Kisses:
Crash, 4

Looking for World War II:
Love & Hunger, An Anthology of New Fiction, Mercury
Press,1988